"Have you ever see~~n anything like this~~, Doc?"

Personally? Chloe had more experience than Chief Ford would know what to do with. "No. I haven't."

Weston shook his head. "How are you holding up?"

"I'm fine." Chloe pointed toward the door, every nerve ending she owned frantic to end the personal conversation between them. The more questions Weston asked, the more she had to lie—and that could get her removed from this investigation.

He headed into the hallway. "There's a diner down the block. I'll be there eating my weight in waffles and bacon if you're hungry."

Chloe followed him to the front door. She had to stay detached from the people here. From Weston. It was the only way to make sure nobody else would be hurt. As soon as she handled the details of the recent victim's remains, she'd get out of town. Move on to the next place. She'd start over.

"Thank you, but I'm—"

The glass door exploded around her, and she hit the floor.

GRAVE DANGER

—

NICHOLE SEVERN

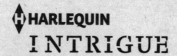

For my babes:

You drive me nuts, but I wouldn't have

it any other way.

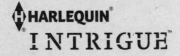

HARLEQUIN®
INTRIGUE™

Recycling programs
for this product may
not exist in your area.

ISBN-13: 978-1-335-48939-5

Grave Danger

Copyright © 2022 by Natascha Jaffa

This edition published by arrangement with Harlequin Books S.A.

For questions and comments about the quality of this book,
please contact us at CustomerService@Harlequin.com.

Harlequin Enterprises ULC
22 Adelaide St. West, 41st Floor
Toronto, Ontario M5H 4E3, Canada
www.Harlequin.com

Printed in U.S.A.

Nichole Severn writes explosive romantic suspense with strong heroines, heroes who dare challenge them and a hell of a lot of guns. She resides with her very supportive and patient husband, as well as her demon spawn, in Utah. When she's not writing, she's constantly injuring herself running, rock climbing, practicing yoga and snowboarding. She loves hearing from readers through her website, www.nicholesevern.com, and on Facebook, @nicholesevern.

Books by Nichole Severn

Harlequin Intrigue

Defenders of Battle Mountain

Grave Danger

A Marshal Law Novel

The Fugitive
The Witness
The Prosecutor
The Suspect

Blackhawk Security

Rules in Blackmail
Rules in Rescue
Rules in Deceit
Rules in Defiance
Caught in the Crossfire
The Line of Duty

Midnight Abduction
Profiling a Killer

Visit the Author Profile page at Harlequin.com.

CAST OF CHARACTERS

Weston Ford—The widower and police chief has learned from his mistakes. Falling in love cost him everything once before, and he's not about to let his growing concern for the town's newest mysterious resident distract him from his job: keeping Battle Mountain safe.

Chloe Pascale—Hiding out in the small remote mining town of Battle Mountain should've been enough for this former cardiothoracic surgeon to start over. But as the threat closes in, she quickly learns changing her name and profession aren't enough to stop the killer she escaped.

Easton Ford—After escaping from Battle Mountain straight into the military when he turned eighteen, Weston's younger brother has finally returned home.

Wesley Byrd—The handyman has more than enough motive to want Chloe dead. Is he the killer burying town residents alive, or is there a bigger game at play?

Battle Mountain—Rocky Mountain mining town comprising 2,800 residents.

Chapter One

Three months ago...

"When I'm done, you're going to beg me for the pain."

Chloe Pascale struggled to open her eyes. She blinked against the brightness of the sky. Trees. Snow. Cold. Her head pounded in rhythm to her racing heartbeat. Shuffling reached her ears as her last memories lightninged across her mind like a half-remembered dream. She'd gone out for a run on the trail near her house. Then... Fear clawed at her insides, her hands curling into fists. He'd come out of the woods. He'd... She licked her lips, her mouth dry. He'd drugged her, but with what and how many milliliters, she wasn't sure. The haze of unconsciousness slipped from her mind, and a new terrorizing reality forced her from ignorance. "Where am I?"

Dead leaves crunched off to her left. Her attacker's

dark outline shifted in her peripheral vision. Black ski mask. Lean build. Tall. Well over six feet. Unfamiliar voice. Black jeans. His knees popped as he crouched beside her, the long shovel in his left hand digging into the soil near her head. The tip of the tool was coated in mud. Reaching a gloved hand toward her, he stroked the left side of her jawline, ear to chin, and a shiver chased down her spine against her wishes. "Don't worry, Dr. Miles. It'll all be over soon."

His voice… It sounded…off. Disguised?

"How do you know my name? What do you want?" She blinked to clear her head. The injection site at the base of her neck itched, then burned, and she brought her hands up to assess the damage. Ropes encircled her wrists, and she lifted her head from the ground. Her ankles had been bound, too. She pulled against the strands, but she couldn't break through. Then, almost as though demanding her attention, she caught sight of the refrigerator. Old. Light blue. Something out of the '50s with curves and heavy steel doors.

"I know everything about you, Chloe. Can I call you Chloe?" he asked. "I know where you live. I know where you work, and I know your running route and how many hours you spend at the clinic. You really should change up your routine. Who knows who could be out there watching you? As for what I want, well, I'm going to let you figure that part out once you're inside."

Pressure built in her chest. She dug her heels into the ground, but the soil only gave way. No. No, no, no, no. This wasn't happening. Not to her. Darkness closed in around the edges of her vision, her breath coming in short bursts. Pulling at the ropes again, she locked her jaw against the scream working up her throat. She wasn't going in that refrigerator like the other victim she'd heard about on the news. Dr. Roberta Ellis. Buried alive, killed by asphyxiation. Tears burned in her eyes as he straightened and turned his back to her to finish the work he'd started with the shovel.

"Don't bother trying to break the ropes. Dr. Ellis learned that the hard way when she dislocated her elbow trying to escape. She suffered for hours before she ran out of air. Needlessly, I might add. If she'd just followed the rules, she would've died peacefully like she was supposed to." *Peacefully.* He said the word as though he'd been doing her colleague a favor when he buried her inside a fridge just like this one. The scrape of metal on rock grated against her nerves. A pile of dirt landed beside her. He was digging a hole, large enough for the refrigerator to fit.

Her grave.

Chloe forced herself to take a deep breath, a combination of chemical cleaner and staleness burning her nostrils. He'd cleaned her makeshift coffin. Police hadn't been able to recover any forensic evidence from inside Dr. Ellis's tomb. It'd been wiped down with bleach before her killer had placed her inside.

She memorized the interior shape of the refrigerator, imagined the door closing on her forever. She had to stall for time. She had to find a way to get free. Scanning the trees and ground around her, Chloe fought to clear her head. Dr. Ellis's body had been buried within the city limits. If the man above her had kept to the same MO, she still had to be in Denver. "If you're going to kill me, why hide behind the mask? Why disguise your voice?"

A combination of dirt and ice froze her from the outside in. Her fingers stiffened. Depending on weather conditions, it took two hours to freeze a body solid. She could still move. They hadn't been out here long. She closed her eyes. She had to focus, listen. Yes, there. A breath of relief rushed from her lungs. Brakes on asphalt, but not a vehicle. Something heavier. A plane? Had her attacker intended to bury her by the airport? If she escaped—

"Oh, I'm not going to kill you, Dr. Miles." The man in the mask rounded back into her vision. Rough hands wrenched her to her feet, and the surrounding forest tilted on its axis. A hint of peppermint dove into her lungs. Gum? "I'm going to let the refrigerator do the job for me. Don't worry. The police will have your location by this time tomorrow, but, one way or another, the truth will come out."

The truth?

"Please, please don't do this. You don't have to do this!" Chloe fought to pull free of his gloved grip, but the ropes around her ankles only unbalanced her. She hit the ground hard. A few inches of soggy foliage softened the blow, but a sharp sliver of rock lodged in her side. A scream escaped her chapped lips. Blood spread across her long-sleeved shirt and jacket as her heart pumped faster.

"Hmm. Well, I don't like that." He stood over her, hands curling into fists. He'd discarded the shovel next to the hole meant to become her grave. "While any injuries inflicted will only make your last moments far more unbearable, that one is going to bleed you dry before I've had a chance to have my fun. But you know that better than anyone, don't you?" Digging into his black cargo pants, he knelt beside her. He produced a small orange plastic box. "Good thing I brought my first-aid kit."

"Go to hell." Covering her wound with both hands, still bound, Chloe locked her jaw against the scream. The rock hadn't gone in too deeply as far as she could tell, but he wasn't getting anywhere near her. Two tugs was all it took to dislodge it from her side, and another moan escaped her control. She quickly set the rock against the ropes around her wrists as he riffled through his small kit.

He laughed. "Every second you waste is another second you're likely to bleed out, Doctor."

The bloodied rock cut through the rope around her wrists faster than she'd expected. Kicking with every ounce of strength she had left, she connected with soft tissue protecting his digestive tract. Pain exploded down her side and across her back, but she shoved it to the back of her mind. Her attacker fell, and she swiped the rock underneath the rope around her ankles before he had a chance to rebalance. She didn't wait to see if he'd gotten up and forced herself to her feet. Chloe pumped her legs hard and ran, her heart in her throat. The main road had to be close. It had to be close.

A growl reached her ears, and she pushed herself harder. Puffs of crystalized air formed in front of her lips. Tears froze in their tracks down her cheeks, the dropping temperatures working to slow her down. She was a runner, but the laceration from her fall on the rock shot agony through her side. Barreling footsteps echoed from behind.

"Help!" she screamed as loud as she could, branches cutting the skin across her neck and face as she raced toward the sound of the road. Her breathing filled her ears. Was that a car passing? "Help!"

The trees started to thin, the light brighter here. Or was that the desperation playing tricks on her mind? Blood seeped through her fingers, but she didn't dare stop. Didn't dare look back. She had to keep going. She had to get to the road.

A wall of muscle slammed her into the icy dirt.

"You're faster than I gave you credit for." His lips pressed into her ear, his breath hot against her over sensitized skin. A shiver raked down her spine, intensifying everything around her. The trees. The roots. He wrapped both hands around one ankle and pulled. "Even when you're bleeding to death. That's why I've always admired you. Your determination. The quality of your work."

All too easily, she imagined Denver police heaving that light blue refrigerator out of the ground after her attacker's anonymous tip and finding her body inside.

"No!" Clamping onto the nearest root, Chloe heaved herself closer to the base of the large pine. The root broke away clean, and her attacker dragged her backward. She couldn't think—couldn't breathe—but she swung as hard as she could.

A groan filled the clearing. His hold on her ankle loosened. She clawed across the foliage. A whooshing sound reached her ears, and she exhaled hard, her tears stinging her cheeks. A car.

Chloe dug her fingernails into the nearest tree and lifted herself to her feet. Run. No looking back. She stumbled forward, gaining strength with every step before she was finally able to jog. Every muscle in her body protested.

Another car drove past. Louder. Closer. Her heart threatened to beat straight out of her chest, but... slower than before. She gasped for air—she was losing too much blood. She could do this. Pressing her hand into her side, she pushed forward. Couldn't stop. He'd catch up any minute. He'd find her. She just had to flag down—

The ground dropped out from under her feet. She rolled end over end. Branches and bushes scratched at her skin as darkness closed in at the edges of her vision. Sliding down the last few feet before the road, Chloe closed her eyes as oxygen crushed from her lungs.

A rumbling tore down the road, growing louder, and she forced her eyes open. No. This wasn't the end. Pain tore through her as she flipped onto her side. She couldn't scream. Couldn't let him find her. "Move, damn it."

A red pickup truck barreled down the road. Chloe struggled to her feet. One step. Two. Asphalt solidified her balance as she raised her hand for the driver to stop. Tires screeched loud in her ears a split second before the darkness swallowed her whole.

Three months later...

THE CALL ABOUT the body had come in a little more than an hour ago.

Police Chief Weston Ford shoved his truck into

Park, the entrance to Contention Mine a soft outline through the windshield. He pulled the flashlight from the glove box and holstered his pistol. It was probably nothing. Teenagers liked to come out here at night. Dare each other to go inside the abandoned mines. It was a rite of passage, proof they weren't kids anymore.

Straw weeds and bushes bent at the wind's whim as he shouldered out of the vehicle. Snow had started melting over the past few weeks, but low temperatures still solidified the dirt under his boots as he surveyed the area. Pressed right into the San Juan Mountains, Battle Mountain, Colorado, and its twenty-eight hundred residents were stuck in the chaotic season shift where the weather couldn't make up its damn mind. It warmed above freezing during the day, but right now, with the sun ducking behind the mountains, ice worked under Weston's thick sheepskin, wool-lined jacket and jeans. He reached back into the vehicle and collected his cream-colored ten-gallon hat, centering it on his head.

He swept his flashlight around the edges of the mine. Up until a few years ago, Contention Mine had been the main source of income for the town and most of the families who lived in it. The owners had been forced to file for Chapter 11 bankruptcy when it became too hard to even purchase toilet paper on credit, but the promise of a fresh start had been enough for town residents to hope. Until things got worse. Battle Mountain coal had supported the economies of two states for decades and fueled a shrinking number of power plants across the country. Now more than six hundred families were out of jobs while the entire town waited for a new company to take over operations.

They'd been waiting six years.

Weston surveyed the footprints in the dirt leading straight into the mouth of darkness. Too many sets to count. The wind rustled through thick pines on either side of the short incline leading into the mine. A low whistle reached his ears from inside. It'd been over a decade since he'd shoveled coal, but the layout had been engrained in his brain a long time ago. He crossed the threshold into pitch-blackness.

Thick supports braced up along either wall and crossed the ceiling above him in expertly measured intervals. The familiar scent of gravel and must dived into his lungs as he searched along the tunnel. His footsteps echoed off the walls the deeper he walked into the mountain. His heart thudded steadily at the base of his skull. None of the kids had waited around for him to show up, most likely terrified of what their parents would think of them crawling around in the deserted mine. But as Battle Mountain's only law enforcement officer, he was duty bound to check it out. In a dying town this small, most of the calls he responded to were domestic violence–related. The unemployment rate had skyrocketed into mid–double digits, stress was higher than ever, tempers raged, and he didn't have time for prank callers.

The ground sloped down. He followed the cart tracks at least three hundred feet. The tension bled from his shoulders, and Weston pulled up short of the slight decline. The flashlight beam vanished about ten feet in front of him. No sign of a body. No sign anyone had come this far into the mine.

"If anyone's down here, I think this is when you're supposed to jump out of the shadows and kill me. No takers? Great." His words tumbled one over the other as they echoed down the length of the shaft. He'd wasted an hour climbing up the mountain and another twenty minutes getting dust and the smell of coal lodged into the fibers of his clothes. "Won't stop me from finding which one of you called in a false report."

He turned back toward the entrance, and a glint of something metallic caught in his flashlight beam. His nerve endings shot into awareness as he maneuvered the beam back. This was a coal mine. Nothing in this mountain should reflect light back like that. Weston closed in on the abnormality. He crouched over a dark patch of dirt. Loose. Disturbed. That didn't make sense. The mine had been shut down six years ago, and he doubted any of the teens in town would spend more time in here than they had to.

The pool of light spread over the patch as he set the flashlight between his teeth and reached for a pen he kept in his jeans. He scooped the metal from the dirt with the end of his pen. It looked like some kind of silver handle, fitting the shape of his hand. Scratches and a couple of dents gouged the worn surface. Mine workers were deliberate about bringing personal effects into the tunnels in case of an accident of the explosive or cave-in variety. Watches, photographs, rings, wallets—anything they could use to be identified in the aftermath. But this length of stainless steel didn't seem to fit the bill. "Now what are you doing down here?"

Weston stepped back, gauging the width and height of the disturbed dirt. Approximately five feet by three feet. Who the hell would come out here to bury something? The hairs on the back of his neck stood on end, and the piece of steel slipped from the end of his pen. He positioned the flashlight near the wall, angling the beam down across the patch of dirt. Unpocketing his phone, he tapped the flashlight button and set his device screen down to cast a wider circle of light. Collapsing, he clawed through the first couple of inches of dirt and scooped it out onto either side of his knees.

He hit something solid.

He hesitated, feeling out the shape of what he'd found with both hands. Following the curve of cold steel, Weston pushed dried, packed dirt out of the way. The smooth surface of the container transformed into a ripple of lettering in the upper right-hand corner. He reached for the flashlight, brushing away as much dirt as he could to read the letters. "Galanz."

A refrigerator?

Warning knotted his gut tighter as he pushed back onto his heels. Something wasn't right. Shoving to his feet, he raced back to the entrance of the cave and out into the frigid temperatures seizing his muscles. He rounded the bed of his pickup and pulled a shovel from the back. Sweat built in his hairline despite the freezing temperatures. His legs protested the exertion as he worked his way back through the tunnel and started digging.

Friction burned his bare hands as he dug out the shape of the rest of the container. There was only one reason someone would come all the way out here to an abandoned mine and bury a refrigerator. No. He couldn't think like that. The call that'd come into the station had to be from one of the teens in town. This was a prank. Battle Mountain was safe. Plunging the end of the shovel into the crevice between the retro-style refrigerator and the wall of dirt around it, he tore his jacket from his shoulders. Something broke away from the door, and Weston angled the flashlight into the shadowed hole.

A padlock.

Swiping his dirt-caked hands under his nose, he

shook his head. Not a prank. Minutes passed. Hell, maybe an hour, but he wasn't going to stop. An ache set up residence in his shoulders as he discarded the last shovel of dirt off to his left. The refrigerator had been set perfectly level within the cocoon of dirt and gravel, the door and freezer box angled straight up toward the ceiling. One foot in the moat he'd shoveled around the container, Weston wedged his fingers between into the rubber seal and pulled.

The gray refrigerator door ripped open and slammed into the earth. Sickening odors escaped, penetrating through the mustiness of the mine as he stepped back. He covered his nose and mouth, but it'd be impossible to forget a smell like that. Decomposition.

He collected his phone from the ground and pointed the flashlight into the container. Air crushed from his lungs as the dust settled around him. Long brown hair coiled around the woman's thin shoulders, dark lashes sweeping across her colorless cheeks as though she were sleeping. Her blue pinstriped shirt and dark jeans followed the contorted shape of her body. The padlock. The burial. The evidence of cracked lips and broken fingernails that had been crusted with blood. A shot of nausea exploded up Weston's throat. It was impossible to get an identification from the swelling around her face and neck, but there was no doubt in his mind. The woman inside the refrigerator had been buried alive. "Holy hell."

He lunged away from the scene and braced himself against one wall as he emptied three cups of coffee from his stomach into the dirt. This wasn't happening. Not in his town. Not like this. Son of a bitch. He had to radio the station. His hands scraped along the walls as Weston stumbled back along the tunnel. The call hadn't been a prank, but his gut said the teens who hung around the mine hadn't been the ones to report the body. They wouldn't have even known it'd been there without unearthing the damn container used to suffocate her.

The killer had made the call.

Weston wrenched open the driver's side door and reached in for the radio strapped to his dashboard. Compressing the push-to-talk button, he tried to force the images he'd seen in that tunnel from his mind. In vain. "Macie, do you copy?"

The radio crackled before the sound clipped short. "Hey, Chief. How's the body hunt going?"

Ignoring the sarcasm in his dispatcher/receptionist's voice, he skimmed the back of his hand across his chin. The soft outline of Contention Mine stared back at him through the windshield, just as it had before. Only this time, a shiver chased down his spine. He'd taken over as police chief three years ago when Charlie Frasier had retired after forty years of protecting Battle Mountain. Nothing like this had

ever happened in their town. He didn't have the resources or the officers for an investigation of this
caliber, but he couldn't ignore the evidence he'd uncovered in that refrigerator. He had a dead woman
on his hands, and he sure as hell was going to find
out who put her there. "I need you to get that new
coroner up here, the one who just moved here. You
know whom I'm talking about. Dr. Pascale."

"Sure, Chief," Macie said. "Did those teens give
you trouble, and you need help getting rid of their
bodies?"

"No." Weston set his forehead against the steering
wheel and closed his eyes. "The call wasn't a prank."

Chapter Two

She was living a lie.

A knot of tension set up residence in her stomach as Chloe hiked the short distance from her vehicle toward the mine's entrance. She wasn't sure why, other than the fact the call that'd pulled her out of bed obviously hadn't been because of natural causes. And she wasn't really a coroner.

She'd gone to medical school, but the license currently hanging in an ornate frame in the smallest back office of the town's funeral home didn't belong to her. Not really. Dr. Chloe Pascale, graduate of University of Colorado's School of Medicine, didn't exist. She'd searched for a graduate name, requested an official copy of their diploma, paid the fee, used her apartment address for the delivery and replaced their name with her assumed identity with the help of some videos online. Chief Ford hadn't questioned her credentials when she'd inquired about the job.

She looked every bit the woman she intended him to see.

The police chief's pickup truck took shape off to her right, the headlights illuminating the dark mouth leading deeper into the mountain. She clutched her medical kit a bit tighter. Macie—Battle Mountain's dispatcher—hadn't been able to tell her much over the phone, but the tone in the woman's voice had revealed the urgency. Chief Weston Ford had discovered a body, and it was her job to investigate the cause of death.

Chloe's boots wobbled on the rough terrain. The small remote mining town was the opposite of everything she'd come to love about Denver. There, she'd had a salary, a support staff, an assistant, an office, family and grocery stores that stayed open past eight o'clock and on Sundays. She hadn't been prepared for the ruggedness of Battle Mountain—the isolation—but escaping to the last place anyone would think to look for her had been her only option. Goose pimples rose along her arms as she stepped into pitch-darkness. "Chief Ford? It's Chloe M— It's Dr. Pascale."

Her voice echoed down the long tunnel. Twice. Three times. Pinpricks of light filtered through the dark, and she put everything she had into shutting out the doubt clawing through her. She buried herself inside her thick coat and fisted the faux-fur collar together with one hand. She'd never been inside a mine before, let alone investigated a body dump. Her nerves shook like the leaves swirling around the entrance to the mine.

"I'm down here, Doc!" The chief's voice hooked into her, tugging her forward.

Chloe took a single step forward, then another. The walls seemed to close in on her all at once, but it was nothing compared to what she'd faced three months ago. She could still envision the exact light blue color of the refrigerator when she closed her eyes. No. She couldn't think about that right now. The chief needed her to ascertain the cause of death on a body left here in the mine. She needed to do the job she'd convinced him she was qualified for when he'd appointed her to the position the first week she'd come to town.

Her fingers tingled as cold set in. She'd been a cardiothoracic surgeon in Denver. She and her team had saved hundreds of lives through life-saving heart transplants, bypasses, stent placements and pacemakers. She could do this. The light at the end of the tunnel separated into two sources. A flashlight and what looked like the light from a smartphone, but she couldn't see much else other than the chief's muscular outline blocking the rest of the scene. Her eyes adjusted slowly. "Macie said you needed me. That you found a body?"

"Yeah. I appreciate you coming all the way out here. I know you haven't been in town long, but I wasn't sure who else to call." Weston craned his head over his shoulder. A few days' worth of beard growth intensified the sharp angles of his face. Dirt stained the waistband of his jeans and the damp white T-shirt clinging to his muscular frame, and she swallowed to counter the punch of attraction coiling through her. Sweat trickled from his short dark hair as he sidestepped around a large hole, giving her a perfect view of what he'd uncovered. "I didn't want to move her."

Everything inside of her went numb.

Blood drained from her face and neck, her entire body heavier than a moment before. She traced the outline of the light gray refrigerator with her gaze, memorized the damage along the edges. Most likely brought on by the shovel in the chief's grip. The dull shape of a padlock—so stark against the darkness of the dirt around the container—claimed her attention. Weston had ripped the door open, exposing the body within, but Chloe couldn't convince herself any of it was real. It couldn't be. She'd escaped. She'd disappeared. This wasn't happening again.

"Doc? You okay? You're looking a little pale." The chief reached out, settling his hand beneath her elbow as though to steady her. His concern battled to counter the ice crystalizing in her veins, but it wasn't enough. It would never be enough. "I have some water in my truck. I'll get it for you."

She didn't want to be left alone with the victim staring back at her.

"No. I'm okay, but thank you." Chloe forced herself to study the woman trapped inside the container, her hands shaking. Long brown hair framed a diamond-shaped face. Warm-toned skin had been drained of warmth upon death and highlighted high-arched eyebrows expertly manicured above the victim's eyes. Lacerations cut through a full bottom lip with the slight hint of bruising along one side of the woman's face. But it was the broken fingernails, painted dark blue and crusted with blood, that stole her voice now. Corresponding scratches were gouged into the interior of the refrigerator door. Chloe motioned to the victim. "Do you... Do you know who she is?"

"I searched her pockets. I didn't find any ID, but in a town this small it's hard not to know everyone who lives here." Weston cleared his throat. "I'll wait for your official report, but I'm almost positive this is Whitney Avgerpoulos. Her family owns the Greek restaurant on Silver Street."

"Did they report her missing?" she asked.

Weston shook his head, grief evident in his expression, in the sinking of his shoulders. "Whitney goes to Colorado Mesa University. She's supposed to be at school right now. She's getting her degree in psychology."

Her heart jerked in her chest as the weight of losing one of his own settled between them.

"I promise to be gentle with her." She'd lived with that same feeling the moment she'd heard of her colleague's murder back in Denver, and she wouldn't wish it on anyone. Chloe unpocketed her phone and tapped the flashlight button. She set down her medical bag. "I'm going to need help removing her from the refrigerator, but before we do that, I need to document the scene."

The chief nodded, a line of determination cutting through his expression. Coming out of his trance, he set the shovel against the nearest wall. "Tell me what you need me to do."

"Can you move your flashlights over her? It'll help with the photos." He did as she asked, and Chloe documented the scene as best she could. Every tap of her phone's camera button echoed around them and punctured through her nerves. She'd gone to medical school, became a surgeon, to help people, to give them a chance. Whoever had put Whitney Avgerpoulos inside the fridge had taken away that chance.

She ensured she'd photographed every inch of the hole Weston had dug around the refrigerator, the container itself and as much detail from the victim as she could. Advancing technology had the capability of seeing more than the human eye. There was a chance her phone had captured something neither she nor Weston could see right now. Crouching, she angled her phone's flashlight to beam from the other side of Weston's, then pulled a tarp from her medical kit. She unfurled the plastic—so loud against the thready pulse throbbing behind her ears—and laid it out flat. "We need to take her out of the refrigerator now."

Weston moved without answering.

Chloe stepped down into the space between the sidewall of the hole and the container, fitting her hands under the victim's right leg and shoulder, as the chief did the same on the other side of the body. They hefted the victim free from the refrigerator and set her gently on the tarp. "I'll collect as much as I can from her hair, fingernails and clothing, but I won't be able to run the tests myself. I have to send it to the Unified Metropolitan Forensic Lab in Denver."

Extracting the sterile cuticle sticks, she ran one each under the victim's broken fingernails and secured them in evidence bags. The weight of Weston's attention pressurized the air in her lungs as he watched from a few feet away. There wasn't anything more she could tell him, nothing she could say that would make the situation easier to process. No matter how much she wanted to. She collected as much evidence from the victim as she could, including a swab of what looked like blood from Whitney's collar. There was a high possibility the sample

belonged to the victim given the state of her lip and
fingernails, but she'd have the lab run it anyway.

"I'm finished." She secured the evidence inside
her medical bag and raised her gaze to the chief's.
"We'll need to get her to my SUV so I can perform
the autopsy back at my office. I should be able to
give you and her family an official cause of death
in the next couple of days." Her "office" was nothing more than a generous description for the town's
funeral home exam room, but it was all she had to
offer.

"Thanks, Doc." Weston didn't move, didn't even
seem to breathe. "I'm not sure I could've done this
without you."

Her gaze wandered to the gray '50s-style refrigerator still half-buried in the earth a few feet away, and
a strike of remembered soreness shot through her.
The mostly healed wound in her side caught fire as
though aware of the thoughts in her head. She'd survived her attacker, made it out of those woods with
some of the same injuries as the woman in front of
her. Her fingers curled into the centers of her palms
as the memory of clawing free from her killer's hold
flashed to the front of her mind. She couldn't ignore
the striking similarities between Whitney Avgerpoulos and herself. The same shade of hair color,
the wide nose and full lips. Based on her heritage,
Chloe could imagine the same color of light green
in the victim's eyes as hers if she were able to see

them. Their skin tones differed, but not enough to set them widely apart. Had the killer come looking for Chloe, only to mistake this woman's identity? She tore her gaze from the scene and fisted both hands in the tarp under the body. "I'm glad I could help."

They moved as one, hauling the victim free from her mountain grave. The chief might not have been able to do this without her, but Chloe couldn't help but wonder if this woman had been killed because of her.

HE'D NEVER HANDLED a homicide investigation before.

In the three years he'd taken over as police chief for Battle Mountain, there hadn't been a single case that'd ended in murder. The preliminary results from the coroner hadn't come back yet, but there was no other way to look at it. Whitney Avgerpoulos hadn't locked herself inside that refrigerator on her own. She wouldn't have destroyed her fingernails trying to claw free if she'd had some part in her own disappearance. No. One of his town's residents had been murdered, and he was going to find out who was responsible.

Weston hiked the short set of stairs leading to the cabin-like home at the end of Bluff Street. The Avgerpouloses's red-brown vertical planking contrasted with the minimalist rock design of the yard. A set of antler horns stood guard over the front door and screen. Despite the desertlike landscaping, the air had a bite to it this early in the morning. He hadn't slept—hadn't eaten—since helping Dr. Pascale get the victim's remains to the funeral home. Not just a victim. Whitney. He'd known Gregory and Delphine Avgerpoulos since they'd arrived in town nearly twenty years ago. Hell, he'd eaten at their restaurant a couple blocks away more times than he could count. He knew these people, but today wouldn't be a social call.

Old hinges protested as he swung the screen wide and rapped on the front door three times. Hints of vanilla and fresh bread in the air filled his lungs from the bakery two streets over. Tall pines and uneven landscape hid his view of the gulch on the other side of the trees surrounding the property on three sides. What the hell was he supposed to say when they answered?

Footsteps shuffled louder from the other side of the wooden door a split second before Gregory Avgerpoulos opened it wide, his dark gaze brightening with an equally matched smile. Aluminum gray hair, peppered with hints of brown, receded halfway down the back of Gregory's shiny head. Thick eyebrows and tanned skin testified to his heritage, but it was the laugh lines branching from either side of his wide nose that caught Weston's attention now. "Chief, to what do we owe the pleasure? Come in, come in." The midsixties father, husband and restaurateur turned back into the house as he cleared the entryway to make room for Weston. "Del! Weston's here."

"Oh, my boy!" Delphine's voice filled the entire house as Weston crossed the threshold just before the woman herself stepped into sight, arms wide. Dark brown hair, coiled in a football helmet of curls, surrounded the woman's head. At nearly six-feet tall, the matriarch of the Avgerpoulos family towered over her husband, but her loud, buoyant personality was what put her over the top. A bright red button-down shirt with geometric patterns in equally bright colors was all he saw just before she wrapped him in one of the most lung-crushing hugs he'd ever experienced. "So good to see you, honey." Pulling back slightly, she pinched his jaw in a strong grip and studied him with deep-set eyes highlighted with bright blue eyeshadow. "It's early. You look like you could use something to eat. Let me get you something."

Weston managed only a few words of protest with his lips squeezed together, but Del ignored every single one of them with two slaps to his cheek. She shuffled into the kitchen as Gregory collapsed into a beat-up recliner as old as he was. The couple had most likely been up for hours.

"No use in fighting her, boy." Gregory's graveled voice reverberated through his chest and rattled slightly. "I think that's how she's gotten me to stay for so long. She just keeps feeding me so I'm too slow to run away."

"I'd take that deal." Weston shut down the urge to relax and removed his hat, pinching the brim between his thumb and index finger. Photographs of the family stared back at him from over the old brick fireplace with brass fixtures. Pictures of Gregory and Del on their wedding day, surrounded by smiling faces. One with Del covered head to toe in the same maroon paint clinging to the walls in this room. The day they opened their Greek restaurant here in Battle Mountain twenty years ago. Baby pictures of Whitney, all the way through elementary school to high school graduation. Weston picked one from the collection. The twenty-two-year-old had an entire life ahead of her after she graduated college. She'd planned on becoming the town's first therapist and helping with the restaurant when her parents needed her. Pressure built under his sternum, and he replaced the photo on the mantel. He wasn't here for lunch. "Have either of you heard from Whitney lately?"

Del danced back into the living room with a plate filled with pita bread, white clumps of cheese, some kind of meat and a whole lot of onion and vegetables. "Not since she visited two days ago. She should be home again on Friday to help with things at the restaurant. We are just so proud of her. Our college girl. Maybe when she is done with her studies, you two can finally go on a date. Neither of you are getting any younger." She set the plate on the small round table separating the living room from the kitchen at the back of the house and pulled out a chair. "Come, sit. You look like death."

"That's very kind of you, but I'm not here for breakfast, Del. I'm here on official business. About Whitney." Weston didn't know how to do this, but he couldn't keep the truth from them. Their daughter—their only child—wasn't coming home.

"Why would you be here about Whitney? She's at school." Gregory locked those small dark eyes on him as Del closed the distance between her and her husband. The old man struggled to his feet, his expression set in hard stone, and gone was the welcoming atmosphere of the family's home. "Spit it out, boy. Tell us what is happening."

"Did something happen to our Whitney?" Del pressed a hand to her chest as though preparing for the worst. She would need the fortification.

"A call came last night around eleven. Someone reported finding a body in the mine. I responded, positive it was just teenagers messing around." Weston dropped his gaze to his hat, unable to face their pain. "But that wasn't the case. I found Whitney."

"No, you're wrong." Anger filled the old man's expression as he shook his head. Gregory shucked off his wife's hand and stepped forward. "That's impossible. Whitney's at school. She went back two days ago. She wouldn't have any reason to be in that mine. You're lying."

"I'm sorry. The coroner and I were able to collect evidence, take photographs and have her remains removed from the container we found her in." A knot of shared grief tightened behind his rib cage, strangling his own breath. "But her dental records from Dr. Corsey confirm it. Whitney is dead."

A high-pitched sob punctured through the living room and set his nerve endings on fire. Delphine Avgerpoulos collapsed, one hand out as though reaching for support, but Weston couldn't force himself to move. Her husband wrapped her in his arms, setting his withered cheek against her mountain of hair.

"I'm very sorry for your loss, Mr. and Mrs. Avgerpoulos." He stepped to the mantel, to the box of tissues, and grabbed the box. After offering each of them a tissue, he took a seat on the edge of a matching recliner next to Gregory's. "I give you my word we're doing everything we can to find out what happened to her, but I need to ask you some questions."

Del nodded, her eyes still closed. "Anything."

"Did Whitney mention any new people in her life, possibly a man you hadn't met yet?" As much as women were capable of murder, it was highly unlikely the person who'd held Whitney down in order to seal her inside the fridge was female. The inclusion of the refrigerator told him the girl's murder had been premeditated. The son of a bitch who'd done this would've had to have been strong enough to haul the damn thing into place before killing his victim.

"No," Gregory said. "No men. Just her friends from school. She has a roommate. We have her phone number on the fridge. Why wouldn't she have called us if Whitney never made it back to school?"

"I'll take her number if you don't mind. I'll be sure to get an account of the last time she saw Whitney." Replacing his hat on his head, Weston unpocketed his notebook and a pen from his coat. "I'll also need the make, model and license plate of her car if you have it and permission to pull her cell phone records."

"What did you mean, you and the coroner removed her from a container?" Del clung to her husband. The gut-wracking sobs were gone now, and a fresh wave of clarity and controlled rage hardened the woman's face. "You ask about new men in her life. You found her in a mine. You collected evidence, you need her car information, you want her cell phone records. Why is all of this necessary?" Del climbed to her feet, staring down at him with promised fire in her eyes. "You tell me the truth, Weston Ford. What happened to our little girl?"

He'd hoped to avoid the details, but they deserved

to know. Meeting her at her level, Weston stood. "The evidence suggests Whitney was murdered."

Del stumbled back a step but refused to go down as Gregory settled back into his recliner behind her. "Who? Who did this to my Whitney? Tell me so I can kill them myself."

"We're not sure yet. I have the coroner examining her now. I'll keep you updated as soon as I have any news. Until then, I need you to call me if you think of any changes in Whitney's life. No matter how small. Understand?" He curled his fingers tighter around his pen. Grief affected people in different ways, and Weston had no doubt in that moment this mother would do as she threatened if given the chance. Hell, he would've done the same if there'd been anyone to punish after his wife had passed, but this wasn't about him. "I'm going to find who did this to her, Del. I'm going to make them pay. I give you my word." He sighed. "Is there someone I can call for you? Your priest or a friend?"

They both shook their heads.

His phone chirped with an incoming call. "I have to take this, but I'll be in touch soon."

Weston left the Avgerpoulos home, kicking up dirt as he headed for his truck. He answered the unidentified number on the fourth ring. "Yeah, this is Ford."

"Chief, it's Dr. Pascale, the...coroner." Her voice wavered with nervousness as she spoke, and he couldn't help but smile at her assumption he'd forgotten her so quickly. "I've just finished Whitney Avgerpoulos's autopsy. There's something you need to see."

Chapter Three

Chloe tore the latex gloves from her hands and deposited them into the hazardous waste basket on the other side of the room. The back room of Jacob Family Funeral Home filled with the chemical odor of a variety of preservatives, sanitizing and disinfectant agents. White upper and lower cabinetry wrapped around two walls of the small space. It wasn't much, but considering there were too few businesses in Battle Mountain willing to handle remains for free, it was all a town this size had to offer.

The steel examination table supporting the remains intensified the colorless pallor of the victim's face and neck exposed by the sheet she'd draped over the body. Chloe studied the sutures holding a perfect Y incision together from shoulder to sternum. Whitney Avgerpoulos hadn't died quietly. While it would take a few days for the samples she'd sent on to the Unified Metropolitan Forensic Lab to render any results, perimortem bruising didn't lie. The victim had fought back. Maybe enough that the killer's identity was somewhere in these samples. Maybe enough to end the nightmare she slipped into every night when she closed her eyes.

"Doc?" The chief centered himself in the doorway, and Chloe stepped back into the corner near one of the cabinets, her heart shooting into her throat. Glass jars stocked with Q-tips, cotton balls and tongue depressors rattled from the impact. Weston raised two sets of coffees as though preparing to approach a wild animal with an offering. The florescent light tubes overhead reflected off the large oval belt buckle at his waist, instantly drawing her gaze down his body. Light stains of dirt dusted the thighs of his jeans and creased his white T-shirt, revealing he hadn't gone home to change since they'd removed the victim's remains from the mine. "Sorry. I didn't mean to startle you. You said you had something for me?"

She shook her head in an attempt to force herself back into the moment and crossed the small preparation room to collect her notes from the other set of cabinets. "Yes. Please, come in, Chief Ford. I just… wasn't expecting you to get here so quickly."

"Not sure if you know this, but it's a small town. It takes me less than five minutes to get anywhere, and you can call me Weston." He stretched one of the coffees toward her. The to-go cup featured the logo of the coffee shop she'd recently discovered on one of her trips through town. Caffeine and Carbs, a combination bakery-and-coffee shop that rivaled the major chain she'd visited in her previous life. "Figured you could use some caffeine. I wasn't sure what you liked, but Reagan assured me your last order was black with two sugars."

"Thank you." Surprise rocketed through her as she took the promise of energy and happiness rolled into one. Her finger interlaced with the chief's for the barest of moments, and a curl of warmth slid through her. Weston had been right. She definitely needed the pick-me-up, considering she hadn't slept since bringing the body back here to the funeral home. The heaviness she'd noted in his body language, the grief that'd contorted his expression in that mine—it'd given her motivation to complete the autopsy as quickly as possible. To give him and the victim's family some kind of answer, but she couldn't ignore the truth. Whoever had attacked Whitney, whoever had buried her in that mine inside a refrigerator, knew Chloe was here.

This victim had been a message.

She wrapped both hands around the cup to chase back the permanent ice of the room. "He remembered my coffee order?"

She read her name written in slanted masculine marker. *Chloe*. Reagan had even spelled it right.

"He remembers everyone's coffee order. I think he keeps notes." Weston pointed to the victim, rounding the other side of the exam table. He worked that chiseled jawline with the press of his back teeth as he studied the young woman's face. "I just had to tell her parents she wasn't coming home from school this weekend. They didn't believe me. Thought I'd made a mistake. She was their only child. Studying to become a psychologist. She was a good kid. Never got into trouble with the law. Parents said she kept to herself, roommate said there hadn't been any major changes in her behavior or schedule recently. She figured Whitney had decided to stay in town to help her parents, which happened a few times now that they're getting older. Didn't mention anyone new in her life, but there has to be a reason someone did this to her."

That same heaviness she'd noted in Weston's voice inside the mine's shaft settled behind her rib cage.

There *was* a reason Whitney Avgerpoulos had been targeted. Because of Chloe.

Fear and shame lodged in her throat. The evidence they'd encountered suggested this murder and the attempt on her life three months ago had to be linked, but detailing her past for a stranger she'd just met shut down the part of her that craved to share her secret. She handed off the file folder with her handwritten notes she'd recorded during the autopsy. "This is everything I was able to determine during the examination, but the main thing I wanted you to see is the puncture wound at the base of her neck."

Setting her coffee on the counter, Chloe tugged a new set of gloves from the flimsy cardboard box and snapped them into place. She motioned Weston around to her side of the table and pressed her index finger just below the puncture mark. "I sent a sample of her blood along with the evidence we collected at the scene for a toxicology screen. There is evidence of a struggle in the perimortem bruising across her face and down her arms, which means it was caused in or around the time of her death. I'm almost positive whoever attacked Whitney sedated her before putting her into that refrigerator, but she fought him." Images of a ring of trees, of the wind on her skin, of lethargy and fear battled to the front of her mind. She straightened, reaching for the coffee cup as though its contents could fortify her against the oncoming storm. "He would've sedated her to get her into the refrigerator. When it wore off—"

"She tried to claw her way out," Weston said.

"Yes." Chloe nodded. "Based on the dimensions of the refrigerator, the victim's size and the evidence of her desperation to get free, I calculated she died of asphyxiation within an hour of waking. The lab can determine what kind of sedative her attacker injected her with. From there, you should be able to trace the drug's purchase to a potential buyer."

"I'm the one who's supposed to protect this town.

How could I have let something like this happen?"
Weston turned away from the examination table,
his head sinking.

"You know as well as I do this isn't something
you could've predicted." Her gut clenched at the
assumed guilt lining the tendons between his neck
and shoulders. Chloe pressed her lower back into
the cabinet behind her for support.

"Is there any way to get a rush on those results?"
he asked.

"I've already put in the request, but the lab is
backed up. They handle over seventy-five percent of
the forensic evidence for criminal cases throughout
the state. It could be a few days, even a few weeks
before we see anything, but I will let you know as
soon as I hear something. The only thing we can do
now is wait." There wasn't much else she could do.
Not here. Her gaze wandered back to the victim.
She'd lost patients before, but there'd always been a
sense of hope before she'd operated. This… There'd
been no hope in this. "Can I ask how you knew she
was out there? According to town gossip, Contention
Mine has been closed for nearly six years."

He didn't turn to face her, his head low.

"Macie took a call at eleven, but the caller
wouldn't give his name. He said there was a body
in the mine. When I got there, I figured it'd just
been kids playing a prank. She's tried calling the
number back, but there's no answer and no record

of anyone registered to that number. I'm working on a warrant for the local usage details. I have a feeling whoever placed the call used a burner." Weston shucked the guilt-ridden exterior and straightened, every ounce the police chief she'd met her first day in town. "Have you ever seen anything like this in all your time as a coroner?"

All of her time as a coroner consisted of two months on the job. In those short few weeks, she'd autopsied one resident who'd died of natural causes. But personally? She had more experience than he would know what to do with. She decided to answer honestly. "No. I haven't."

Weston shook his head. "How are you holding up? Can't imagine you've gotten much sleep or anything to eat since last night."

The question knocked her control off balance. One of his town's residents had been murdered, but he wanted to know how she was holding up? Terrified, isolated, helpless—all the same emotions she'd experienced when she'd woken in the hospital after her attack. Only tenfold. This wasn't just about her anymore. Another victim had been killed. One tied to the new town she'd run to hide in. Chloe tossed her unfinished coffee in the trash and ripped the latex gloves from her hands before shoving them in her lab coat pocket. "I was going to go home and catch a couple hours of sleep after I finished here. I won't be able to release her remains to her family until the investigation is concluded, but I'll make sure Mr. Jacob takes good care of her while she's here."

"You're good at dodging personal questions, Doc, but considering you look as beat as I feel, I'll let it slide." Weston tossed his to-go cup into the same trash can, a hint of aftershave and dirt cutting through the smell of embalming fluid, which was a permanent part of this establishment. "Have you at least eaten anything?"

"I'm fine." She pointed toward the door, every nerve ending she owned frantic to end the personal conversation between them. The more questions he asked, the more she had to lie, and lying to him could get her removed from this investigation. There had to be a connection between her attack and this murder, but she wouldn't put anyone else's life at risk to find it. "I grabbed a bag of chips from the vending machine at the front a couple hours ago. There are still a few left in the bag if you're interested."

"Breakfast of champions." He headed for the door and into the hallway. "There's a diner down the block. Greta's on Main. Great food. I'll be there eating my bodyweight in waffles and bacon for the foreseeable future if you're still hungry."

Chloe followed him through the building, past the casket showroom and to the front door. She had to stay detached from the people here. From him. It was the only way to make sure nobody else would get hurt. As soon as she handled the details of Whitney Avgerpoulos's remains, she'd get out of town. Move on to the next place. She'd start over. "Thank you, but I'm—"

The glass door exploded around her, and she hit the floor.

HER SOFT EXHALE brushed against the underside of his jaw.

Weston tried to keep his weight off her, but the force with which he'd tackled her to the floor had pinned her beneath him. A waterfall of brown hair tangled in his hands as he searched her face for the slightest sign of distress. The edge of her thick dark eyebrows met over the bridge of her nose and deepened the small vertical line between them. Pale green eyes searched their surroundings as she set her hands against his chest, and an explosion of adrenaline and concern combined into a vicious tornado of emotion. Someone had just shot at them. "Tell me you're okay."

"Kind of hard to breathe." Full pink lips parted as she pressed against him.

"Oh, sorry." Weston rolled off her and shoved to his feet. He offered her a hand, locking his jaw against the comfort of her soft gold skin, and tugged her to her feet. Their breaths mixed in the small space between them before he forced himself to release her. Glass crunched under his boots as he surveyed the damage. A frigid burst of air raised the hairs on the back of his neck. "Stay here."

He wrenched what was left of the glass door open and stepped out onto Main Street. A few parked vehicles. Little movement. Fragments of startled conversation and worried faces filtered in from his peripheral senses as he jogged into the middle of the road. No sign of the shooter. No vehicle leaving the scene. His heart caught in his throat. Whoever had shot at them was already gone. He twisted around, facing the residents hugging against the walls of the fly shop and the small internet café on either side of the funeral home. "Is everybody okay? Is anyone injured?"

Terror contorted the faces of the townsfolk, but no sign of injuries. He'd gather statements as soon as he determined they were all safe.

Footsteps echoed from behind as Frank Jacob Sr., the funeral home director himself, lurched to a stop on the sidewalk outside the property. "Chief, I heard the shot from the back room. What's going on? Is there anything I can do?"

Details raced through his mind. Less than eight hours ago, he'd uncovered the remains of a young woman. Now this. It couldn't be a coincidence. Whitney Avgerpoulos's murder and the shooting had to be connected. Whoever had targeted the funeral home obviously hadn't wanted an investigation into her death. They would've known he'd brought the victim's remains here, where the coroner worked. The bastard must've followed him from the mine, which meant… "Chloe."

She brushed pieces of broken glass from her white lab coat and stumbled from the shattered remains of the front door.

The homicide investigations he'd studied over the years had all had a similar theme. Murderers would do whatever it took to ensure they weren't caught. If Whitney Avgerpoulos's killer had gotten word Weston had taken the case, there was a chance the perp would target anyone involved. Including the coroner who'd collected evidence from the remains. He charged back onto the sidewalk. "Mr. Jacob, I need you to secure Whitney Avgerpoulos's remains as soon as possible. Move them to another location if you have to, but I want them under lock and key."

"I don't understand." The thin aging director's hollowed cheeks sank a bit deeper as confusion set in. "What's going on?"

"I don't have time to explain. Please, make sure nobody but you has access to her or any evidence Dr. Pascale hasn't forwarded to the lab until we figure out who took that shot," he said. "I'll have someone from Hopper's start working on your door as soon as I can. Until then, make sure everyone here is okay, and send them to the station to give a statement to Macie."

"I'll do what I can." Frank Jacob strode back into the funeral home.

Frantic questions penetrated through the ringing in his ears as he closed the distance between him and Chloe. *Chief, what happened? Who would do this? Are we in danger?* Damn it. He didn't have answers, but it was only a matter of time before the town learned of Whitney's murder and the wildfire of rumors would spread. This was already getting out of control. He slid his hand between the doc's rib cage and arm, directing her to his pickup parked down the street. "Come on. I need to get you out of here."

"You think this is related to Whitney Avgerpoulos's murder." She quickened her step to keep up with him as he pulled her down the street past Hopper's Hardware. "That whoever killed her might be targeting us to keep us from solving the case." Her voice remained even despite the fact they'd just survived a shooting. How the hell was that possible under the circumstances when it took everything in him not to panic? "You can drop me off at my apartment. I'll pack a bag and check in to the hotel."

Weston wrenched open the passenger side door of his truck and deposited her inside. Townspeople called after him as he rounded the front of the pickup and collapsed behind the wheel. The twenty-year-old engine growled to life, and he ripped away from the curve, heading straight out of town. His position required him to gather statements from witnesses and collect evidence, but all he could think about was Chloe's safety. "You can't go back to your apartment or to the funeral home. Whoever pulled the trigger might already know where you live. As of this moment, you're officially under Battle Mountain PD protection."

Main Street shops bricked in various shades of red and thick clusters of winter-stripped trees blurred in his peripheral vision as they left the town limits. Snow-capped peaks demanded attention as they headed west. His heart pounded behind his ears as he fought the onslaught of adrenaline.

"And by Battle Mountain PD, you mean you. Alone," she said.

"Not alone, really. Macie has her concealed carry permit." The weight of her attention told him adding Macie into the mix hadn't helped his case, and she was right. Battle Mountain didn't have the resources of Grand Junction, where she'd come from, or any of the bigger cities across the state, but this small mining town was all he had. As much as he wanted the truth to be different, there was no changing their reality. He wasn't real law enforcement. He'd taken the role of police chief after no one else in town had been willing to step up when Charlie Frasier suffered a heart attack on the job. In the eyes of the town, he was the one responsible for protecting every man, woman and child in and out of these town limits. Hell of a job he was doing so far, but just because he hadn't gone to the academy, didn't mean he wasn't capable of keeping Chloe safe.

"Okay, so you and your dispatcher." That sense of calm he'd noted earlier cracked on her last word and sucker punched him straight to the gut as though she'd physically hit him. "No offense, Chief, but have you or Macie worked an active shooter or homicide investigation before?"

"No." He took his eyes off the road ahead to glance in her direction. "Have you?"

The doc pulled her shoulders back, sitting a bit straighter in her seat. Sun cut through the back windshield of the pickup and highlighted the barely evident birthmark on her chin. "No. The people I work with are usually victims of those two scenarios."

"I guess that makes us even." Weston gripped the steering wheel tighter. "You and I are the only two people who know what really happened to Whitney Avgerpoulos, and we're the only two who can bring her killer to justice. Her parents deserve to know what happened to their little girl. I can't do this without you, Doc."

Chloe directed her attention out the passenger side window and up the jagged peaks of the San Juan mountains. Hints of her perfume still clung to his T-shirt and jacket and filled the cabin of the truck. Something complex, mysterious even. Bright citrus notes and a smooth touch of bourbon that caught in his throat. Hell, he'd never smelled anything like it and wanted to drown in it. A crushing wall of apprehension slammed into him as she turned in her seat to face him. "I was able to ship the samples I collected from the mine and the victim's remains to the forensic lab just before you arrived. Lucky for us, I got everything I could from her before the shooting, but we won't be able to get a conviction if her remains are compromised. I heard you tell Mr. Jacob to move her to a secure location. As long as he follows instructions, you'll have a case. I've done my job. You don't need me."

Instinct raised goose bumps on the back of his arms, and Weston pulled the truck to the side of the road. Dirt kicked up alongside both doors and clouded the view behind them. Draping one hand over the steering wheel, he faced her, memorized her expression, the slight changes in her breathing.

"What are you doing?" she asked.

"I've been working under the impression that bullet was meant for me. Tell me I'm wrong." Something was off. He might not have been officially trained in law enforcement, but he trusted his gut plenty of times to get him out of trouble. And right now, his instincts were screaming she hadn't been honest with him all this time, that she was hiding something. In all the times he'd asked her a personal question or tried to get to know her these past few weeks, she'd given him a sarcastic answer or changed the subject entirely.

She didn't move, didn't even seen to breathe.

Her reaction in the mine flashed through his memory. According to the degrees hanging at the back of the funeral home, she was a coroner. She dealt in death, but he'd watched the blood drain from her face when she'd gotten a good look at Whitney Avgerpoulos's body in that refrigerator, noted the tremor in her hands. At the time, he'd pushed it off as nothing more than exhaustion, but now… "I was so worried that I might've put you in danger by dragging you into this investigation, I didn't stop to think why this was happening in the first place. Battle Mountain hasn't seen a homicide investigation in over thirty years, but within weeks of you coming to town, I've had to pull a body out of a mine and nearly got shot for my trouble. You know something."

"You're wrong. I don't know who's doing this or why someone shot at us." She shook her head, gazed out the windshield as though working out a way to escape. "I don't know why this keeps happening to me."

Air stalled in his chest. "What do you mean?"

She curled her lips between her teeth and visibly bit down, drawing a bead of blood. "I think whoever killed Whitney is the same person who tried to kill me."

Chapter Four

She hadn't said the words before. Not out loud.

The weight of Weston's attention pressurized the air in her lungs. She didn't know what else to say, what to do. Whoever'd abducted and buried Whitney Avgerpoulos in that refrigerator had followed her from Denver. It would be too much of a coincidence otherwise.

"We need to get off the main road." After sending a text on his phone, Weston slid his grip to the bottom of the pickup's steering wheel and put the truck in Drive. A blanket of dust kicked up behind them in her passenger side mirror, blocking her view of Battle Mountain, and the hollowness in her chest expanded. "I know a place. Once we're out of town, you're going to tell me everything."

Chloe nodded.

They turned onto an unpaved road a little outside town and wound through a combination of mountainous ridges and family-owned ranches. Dropping temperatures seeped through the vehicle's windows, and she burrowed inside her coat. She hadn't come out this way before, too aware of the openness, the exposure of leaving the town limits, but she couldn't help soak it all in. In all her years in Denver, she'd rarely left the comfort of the city, with its skyscrapers, clean lines and detachment from nature. But this… Her fingers tingled with the urge to brush her hands through the dense pines climbing higher along the ridge steps of the mountain, to breathe in their fresh scent, to forget.

Serrated peaks fought to pierce the bright blue sky. A gaggle of geese called over rocky canyons and high valley floors. A crystalline river flowed alongside the dirt road, promising adventure and endless exploration, before it widened into an impossibly green-blue lake nestled in a small valley. No matter where she looked, the magic captivated her all over again, and a sense of belonging solidified in her stomach. "It's stunning."

"It's home," Weston said.

Time distorted into a warm, wondrous fluid as they climbed higher, but just when she didn't think they could go any farther, another valley spread out in front of them. She wasn't sure how long they'd been driving, didn't care. She couldn't remember the last time the world had been this beautiful.

Momentum pushed her forward in her seat as Weston turned once more up a long dirt drive. They passed beneath the behemoth logs supporting the large sign over the entrance to the fenced property reading Whispering Pines Ranch. The pickup rocked back and forth as they headed toward a large log cabin surrounded by a ring of massive trees. A herd of deer raised their heads at their approach up the driveway. A bright green roof and trim set the structure apart from the smaller satellite cabins located less than a few hundred yards in each direction, but Chloe didn't understand. He'd told her he was taking her out of town, somewhere safe. "What is this place?"

"Welcome to Whispering Pines. Nine hundred acres of wilderness, lakes, wildlife and…" Weston pointed out the windshield as a white-haired woman stepped down from the front porch of the main cabin. Another outline, a man equal in age to his counterpart, left the shade provided by the wraparound porch and secured a hand on the woman's shoulder with a wave of his own. The chief raised two fingers from the steering wheel in greeting. "…them."

"I don't understand. Who are they?" Hesitation tightened the tendons between her shoulders and neck as the truck pulled to a stop.

"My parents, Karie and James Ford." Weston cut the engine, and a bite of nervous energy skittered down her spine. "Come on. If I don't introduce you, they'll pull you out of the truck themselves."

Chloe gripped the passenger door handle and forced herself from the vehicle. A finger of cold worked under her coat as Weston rounded the front of the truck and met the older couple halfway. He secured his mother in a tight hold, and Chloe's stomach flipped at the obvious warmth between them. James Ford shook his son's hand before bringing him in for a one-armed hug, and a responding smile creased her lips. Nervous energy spun in a chaotic funnel behind her sternum as she suddenly realized she was intruding on an intimate reunion. This was the chief's family, his home, his land. Why would he bring her here?

"Mom, Dad, this is Dr. Pascale. She's the new coroner in town." Weston extended an arm toward her, a renewed brightness in his gaze. "Doc, these are my parents. They'll be doing everything in their power to get the two of us to settle down and give them grandchildren."

"Someone has to." Karie Ford hit her son with the back of her hand against his chest, and he feigned injury. The Ford matriarch closed the distance between them, extending one hand. Callouses scraped against Chloe's palms as the woman studied her up and down. Ear-length white-gray hair turned out at the ends effortlessly, framing a delicate jaw and piercing brown eyes, but there wasn't much else delicate about Karie Ford. Dark jeans and a flannel shirt with a fitted T-shirt underneath highlighted lean muscle that could only come from decades of working the land around them. Her laugh lines deepened around her eyes and mouth as she smiled. Dirt stained unpolished short nails, but the contact of this woman's hand in hers settled Chloe's nerves faster than a straight black cup of coffee. "It's so nice to meet you, Dr. Pascale. Weston has told us a little bit about you since you came to town, but he didn't tell me how beautiful you are."

Her gaze cut to Weston. He had? A series of internal tremors rocked through her at the thought. The chief had been discussing her with his parents. "Chloe is fine, and thank you for letting me visit. It's nice to meet you."

"Visit? No, dear. Weston messaged us and said your apartment wasn't safe until you two figure out who killed that poor girl. You're staying with us. After what happened at the funeral home, I imagine you could use a good meal and some sleep." Karie released her hand and called over her shoulder. "You got it all set up, right, James?"

"Yes, ma'am. You're welcome to stay as long as you need in Weston's old cabin." The head of the Ford family stepped into her peripheral vision. Unkempt gray hair swung into James Ford's eyes. Similarly dressed as his wife, Weston's father nodded at her with a finality in his voice, a grumble that could soothe the most terrifying situations. Thick beard growth worked to mask the ranch owner's age, but the set of forehead wrinkles put him somewhere in his sixties as far as Chloe could tell.

"Then it's settled. As long as there is a psychopath in these parts, you're ours," Karie said. "And you're just in time. Lunch is almost ready. Hope you like corn chowder. It's Weston's favorite, and since he's too busy policing the entire town to visit his parents, I figured I'd try to lure him to come back more often."

The low rumble of James's laugh battled to penetrate through her panic.

Another bolt of hesitation flooded through her, but the Fords were already maneuvering her up the main cabin's front porch steps and into the warmth of the family home. A killer had followed her from Denver to Battle Mountain, and the first place Weston could think to take her was his family home? Chloe glanced back toward him for a sign of what she should do, but the police chief only smiled back with compliance. There would be no argument.

Heat enveloped her the moment she stepped over the threshold. A massive stone fireplace climbed two stories up the open main living space. Light grade wood, lighter than the exterior of the cabin, absorbed the sunlight penetrating through floor-to-ceiling windows on one end of the home. A frayed multicolored crocheted rug took up a majority of the hardwood floor. A small carved bear holding a bowl of fruit claimed her attention from the table stretching the back of the dark leather sofa. Similar carvings had been strategically positioned around the open kitchen and against the grand staircase leading to the second level. Handcrafted lamps, varying shades of animal fur and muted nature paintings finished the space in old-style hunter decor. It was perfect in every way. It was a home.

The scents of pepper, cream and potatoes filled her senses as Chloe took it all in, and her stomach revolted against the single bag of chips she'd gorged herself on hours ago. But as much as she wanted to sink into one of the leather sofas with a bowl full of soup and soak in all the warmth Karie and James Ford offered while she forgot the fact that Whitney Avgerpoulos's killer might've come to Battle Mountain for her, she couldn't. Not without putting the police chief and his family at risk. "If you don't mind, I'd like to use your restroom to freshen up."

"Follow that hallway, first door on the left." James vaguely motioned toward the stairs as he stirred the steaming pot of chowder.

Weston studied her from the end of the kitchen island as his mother handed over plates, spoons and bowls to set the massive wooden family table, but she couldn't focus on him right now. The longer she stayed here, the more danger she'd put him in.

Her boots echoed off the hardwood as she followed the hallway through the main level and stepped into the bathroom. She secured the door behind her and locked it, instantly relieved at the sight of the large square window over the Jacuzzi-style tub. Climbing into the tub, Chloe unlatched the window and slid the pane back on its tracks slower than she wanted to go to keep them from protesting. She knocked the screen out and hauled one leg through, then the other. A jolt of impact rocketed through her as she hit the ground. It would be a long and risky trek back to Battle Mountain, but she'd left her car at the funeral home and her go bag with supplies in her apartment. She had to take the chance. Chloe crept along the side of the house and rounded the corner to the front.

Weston crossed his arms over his muscular chest as he settled against the hood of his truck, and she froze. "Now where do you think you're going?"

"YOU AND I weren't able to finish our earlier conversation." Weston shoved off the hood of his pickup, closing the distance between them. Chloe's gaze darted to the driveway off to his left, and amusement hooked into him. "If you're thinking about running again, I have to warn you. I know every inch of this land. You won't make it more than half a mile before I catch up to you."

Her throat flexed with a hard swallow. "I told you I believed the person who killed Whitney Avgerpoulos was the same man who attacked me, and you bring me straight to your parents' house. The longer

I stay here, the more danger they are in, and they don't deserve to suffer because of me. Neither do you. I'm going back to town. I'm going to get as far from here as possible and give you an escape from this nightmare before more people end up hurt. Or worse, dead."

"First, my parents can take care of themselves. If you don't believe me, just wait until you see my mom peg a coyote from three hundred yards." He stepped toward her, cutting off her view of the driveway and forcing her to meet his gaze. "Second, whoever killed that girl did it in my town, and as police chief, it's my job to bring him to justice. Third, I brought you here because it was the safest place I knew. Every member of my family believes in the second amendment, and they are not afraid to exercise that right. Our killer might be smart enough to connect me to the investigation and this place, but he'd be an idiot to try to come here for you. You're safe here, Doc. I give you my word. But in order to protect you, I need to know what happened before you came to Battle Mountain."

Her lips thinned as she shifted her weight between both feet. She was beginning to break, the circles under her eyes darker than before. Hell, it seemed like a lifetime ago they'd pulled Whitney's remains from that mine. Not nine hours. Time flew when being shot at. Chloe lowered her chin to her chest and kicked at the dirt around her with one boot.

"My name isn't Chloe Pascale. It's Chloe Miles, and I'm not a coroner from Grand Junction. I lied after… I am—was—a cardiothoracic surgeon out of the heart and vascular center in Denver. I was in the middle of a run in the woods near my house when he ambushed me." She shoved her hands in her coat pockets, still unwilling to meet his gaze. "Three months ago, I woke up in the middle of a clearing. He was there, digging a hole. I didn't recognize him because of the ski mask, but I remember it was cold. I couldn't feel my toes or my fingers or process what was happening. Until I saw the light blue refrigerator a few feet away."

A refrigerator. The same kind the killer had used to bury Whitney? Weston's instincts shot into awareness. The puncture wound on the victim's neck. Chloe had known to look for it because she'd been in Whitney's position. "He drugged you."

"I can't be sure with what, but my best guess is with propofol, yes." Chloe relaxed her shoulders away from her ears and finally lifted her attention to him. "The injection knocked me out almost immediately, but the sedative has a short half-life, and the effects don't last long. It doesn't show up in standard urine tests or toxicology results. I imagine he specifically chose propofol for those reasons. He had to work fast to get me into the refrigerator, but once I was inside, I'd know exactly what was happening. He wanted me to be aware of every second up until

I ran out of air, and when my body was discovered, the medical examiner wouldn't be able to tell what I was sedated with." Chloe took a step back. "It was a good plan, one that would've worked if I hadn't fought back, but now he's in Battle Mountain. He knows I'm here, and he killed that girl to make sure I got the message this isn't over."

Hell. He'd have to deal with her deception at some point. He'd appointed her under false pretenses, and his duty to the town meant he'd have to consider the consequences of her lies. Right now, though, he needed to focus on protecting her. Weston countered her escape and wrapped his grip around both of her arms. "He's not going to lay another hand on you, Doc. Not as long as I'm part of this investigation. Okay? We're going to figure out who killed Whitney. We're going to make him pay. Together."

"How? We don't have the resources to run the samples I took from the victim's remains ourselves. I'm a former surgeon, not police, and you're the only law enforcement officer in this town." She swiped at her face, a rattle of a sob entwining with her words. "He's killed two people now, including one of my colleagues. How are we supposed to do this alone?"

Whitney wasn't the first victim? Damn it. She was right. He didn't have the resources of a full-fledged department to connect all the spiraling pieces of this case, but there was a chance they'd get at least a description of their shooter from witness statements or some kind of lead from reviewing that first case. But the priority had to be Chloe for now. His gaze flickered to the satellite cabin farthest from the main house, and his gut knotted tighter. He hadn't spoken to the man on the other side of the door in months, but it was worth a shot. Chloe was right. They couldn't do this alone. He slid one hand down her arm and cupped her hand in his. Weston tugged her after him. "I have someone who can help—my brother."

She fought to keep up with his steps.

He banged on the cabin's wood front door, removing his hat out of respect. Footsteps echoed from inside a split second before a wall of muscle and hostility filled the frame. Weston released Chloe's hand, standing a bit straighter, but even at six-one, his brother outranked him by more than three inches. "Easton."

Several days' worth of stubble softened the sharp, angular jaw underneath. Two distinct lines furrowed between Easton's eyebrows as the former Green Beret stared down at him for a fraction of a second before turning that detached gaze on the woman at his side. Unkempt hair and the odor of sweat and staleness revealed the soldier Weston had once admired wasn't taking care of himself here at home any better than he had been in the Middle East. Easton folded broad arms across his chest and leaned against the doorjamb. "Who's this?"

The muscles down Weston's spine hardened with battle-ready tension at the hint of disrespect in his younger brother's voice. "This is Chloe. She's the new coroner in town, and we need your help."

"I didn't realize Weston had a brother." Chloe rubbed her palm down her jeans before stretching it out in greeting. "Nice to meet you."

The hostility intensified as seconds distorted into silent minutes. The soldier pushed off the doorjamb and stepped back into the house. Shadows cut across his neutral expression as he slammed the door shut in their faces.

Disappointment and frustration tornadoed in his chest as Weston stepped off the cabin's small front porch. He replaced his hat on his head. He should've known six months back home wouldn't be enough to introduce Easton back into the real world, but he wasn't about to give up. Not on family.

"I take it your brother is more of the strong, silent type," Chloe said.

Weston retraced their steps back toward his pickup, then farther to the cabin his parents had cleaned out for Chloe. The rustic exterior matched the main house apart from the shade of trim framing the front door, a single window and the roof. With six satellite cabins, plus the main house, his parents had managed to raise a family and build a successful guest ranch for tourists looking to get the real experience of mountain living. Including the ill-tempered bear he'd called his brother all his life.

"Easton is former Special Forces. He and his unit were almost single-handedly responsible for rooting out terrorists and insurgents in Afghanistan and Iraq during the war." A note of sobriety tinted his voice as his frustration with Easton's behavior faded. "He doesn't like to talk about it, or talk in general, or leave his cabin, but from what the army has been able to tell us, he's the only one who made it home."

"I'm sorry to hear that," Chloe said. "I can't imagine how hard that must be."

Weston twisted the knob and shoved inside. The door swung back into the handmade shelves he'd installed years ago above the single-countered kitchen to the left. A small square dining table matching the same wood as the cabin floor angled off to one side, leaving room for him and Chloe to pass into the living room. A queen-size bed had been positioned under the second window at the back left corner, and exhaustion suddenly drained the last remnants of his energy dry. "It's not much, but you're welcome to stay here as long as you need."

Her gaze roamed over the small one-room space, and Weston suddenly found himself memorizing the small changes in her expression. She shucked her heavy coat and hung it on one of the three hooks beside the door at the same time as the heat from the fire hit him full force. His parents had taken good care of this place, wiping any and all surfaces clean of dust, but the memories were still engrained at the back of his mind. Her boots echoed off the hardwood as she moved through the kitchen, fingers brushing the sleek granite countertop on either side of the sink. "This was your cabin?"

"Up until about three years ago." He surveyed the room, hands on his hips, taking it all in again. "Once I took up as police chief, I figured I needed a place closer to town. Mom and Dad rent it and the other four available cabins out to tourists now. Keeps them busy and gives them something to focus their parental nagging on."

Her laugh drove into the spaces between the massive logs holding this place up and his nerve endings caught fire. "My parents both passed away when I was in med school, but I still remember their constant check-ins. Making sure I did my laundry, that I was staying on top of my studies, questioning me about any men I'd started dating. And I lived on campus. I couldn't imagine having them any closer than that until I found myself wishing I'd answered more of their calls before their car slid off the road one night." She moved to the kitchen drawers, pulling them out one by one, and lifted what looked like a framed photo from inside. She turned the frame toward him. "Now I can definitely tell this was your cabin, but who's the woman next to you?"

Air crushed from his lungs as recognition burned

through him. He stood a bit taller without needing to see the photo to know exactly whom he'd been standing beside when it'd been taken. "Her name is Cynthia. She's my wife."

Chapter Five

His wife.

The words echoed in her head even as her gaze dipped to the bare ring finger of his left hand. Chloe forced herself to set the heavy frame back in the drawer where she'd discovered it and swiped her hands down her jeans. She hadn't expected the knot of disappointment to hit so hard, as though she'd physically taken a sucker punch to the stomach. The kindness Weston had shown her and the invitation to breakfast before a bullet had almost penetrated her skull hadn't been out of interest. He treated everyone with the same amount of respect and warmth. Wow. As much as she'd told herself personal connections would complicate her situation, the hollowness behind her sternum flared. How could she have been so stupid? "I…I didn't realize you were married."

"Would've been four years this past December." Weston closed the distance between them and reached past her into the drawer where she'd set the photo. He swiped a thin film of dust from the glass with the sleeve of his jacket, filling the space between them with a floating array of airborne glitter. Staring down at the blonde beauty in the photo, the police chief angled the photo toward her. "We'd only been married a few months when she was diagnosed. Lymphoma. Her dad had been diagnosed the year before. He managed to pull through, but Cynthia…"

Dread pooled at the base of her spine, and her heart jerked in her chest. "She didn't survive," she said on a whisper.

"No. Her doctors did everything they could. We all did, but the chemo and the cancer itself was too much for her to handle." Weston sniffed as he lowered the frame to his side. He turned, scanning the rest of the cabin as though willing to look at anything but her, and set the photo on the small dining table in the middle of the room. "I didn't realize this was still here. I'll check the rest of the place to make sure my parents didn't leave anything else like this around."

Chloe took a single step toward him. "I didn't know."

"It was a long time ago," he said.

But the scar still lingered in his mesmerizing brown eyes. Grief was frustrating like that, rising and falling in a flood of sadness and detachment before disappearing for a while. One trigger. That was all it could take to reignite the despair and widen the hole where the person you loved had carved out space in your heart. As much as she'd pushed off her parents' constant concerns and their pressure for her to succeed as a Latina woman in a male-dominated field, she'd loved them. She missed them. At least she'd had someone to worry about her, to love her. Now, she had no one.

"Before, you said Whitney Avgerpoulos isn't the only victim in this case, that whoever killed her killed one of your colleagues." Weston hooked both thumbs into his front pockets, exaggerating broad shoulders and muscled arms beneath his sheepskin coat. "From what I've studied from some other department case files, the more victims there are in a homicide investigation, the higher chance of recovering evidence that leads to the killer's identity. Sooner or later, they make a mistake."

The investigation. Right. Chloe swallowed past the dryness in her throat, forcing herself back into the moment. "I'm not sure how much help I can be. It was mostly on the news, but I knew the first victim. She was an anesthesiologist in the hospital where I worked. Dr. Roberta Ellis. She sedated a number of my patients during surgery up until about four months ago when she stopped showing up for her shifts."

"Was that like her?" Weston's voice dipped into neutral territory. No hint of the controlled grief cracking through his expression.

"No. She never missed a shift. She was interviewing at larger hospitals a few weeks before her disappearance. She loved working with us as far as I knew, but Roberta wanted to take on more shifts, and we didn't have the resources at the time. When she didn't show up for two of my surgeries, I assumed she'd moved on to another job. Until I recognized her photo on the news." Chloe folded her arms across her chest as the memories charged forward. "Police received an anonymous tip about a body in Washington Park. When they arrived, they found a handle from a refrigerator lying on top of a recently disturbed patch of soil. The reporters had gotten footage from the crime scene. There was a yellow refrigerator in the hole they'd excavated. Later, I learned she'd been buried alive inside of it."

"And when you woke up in that clearing three months ago and saw a similar refrigerator a few feet away, you believed you'd been targeted by the same killer." Weston's footsteps reverberated through the hardwood floor and up her legs as he closed the distance between them.

She hugged herself a bit tighter, a sting of awareness bristling from the mound of scar tissue under her clothing. "I didn't want to be his next victim. That's the only thing that kept me going."

"Did you go to the police? Were they able to find the scene where he intended to bury you?" Weston asked.

"I gave them everything I could remember. How he'd ambushed me, how I escaped, what his voice sounded like. The driver who nearly hit me with his truck was even able to pinpoint exactly where he picked me up, but the search teams didn't find anything. My doctors informed the detectives who took my statement that I'd been sedated." A bubble of renewed fear closed in, and her blood pressure spiked. "After that, they discounted me as a reliable witness, and anything I had to say wouldn't only be inadmissible in court, but a risk the district attorney wasn't willing to take. But he was still out there."

"They dropped the investigation, and you ran. You changed your name and came to Battle Mountain. Hell." Weston scrubbed a hand down his face. "I'll send my notes to the original detectives and request the investigation files from Denver PD. There are too many similarities between your colleague's and Whitney's murders for us to think these cases aren't connected. They might not have had the evidence to pursue your case, but they won't be able to ignore another body." He wrapped his hands around her arms, just as he'd done outside, and a flare of warmth penetrated through the permanent ice that'd set up residence since her attack. "I'll make sure of it."

She stared up at him, and time stretched from one minute to the next. A coil of appreciation tightened inside her the longer he held on to her. It'd been months since she'd had someone to talk to, someone to listen. While the nightmares and persistent fear of her attacker closing in had weakened her over the past three months, Chloe felt as though Weston stood as a wall of physical and mental protection in a killer's path. "Thank you."

His hands slid down her arms, and Weston stepped back. He narrowed his gaze on hers. "You said you and the first victim, Roberta Ellis, worked in the same clinic? A heart and vascular center in Denver."

"Yes," she said. "Roberta was an anesthesiologist, and I was in cardiothoracic, but we frequently worked together during surgery."

"Did you or Roberta ever hang out outside of work?" he asked. "Did she ever say anything to you about feeling like she was being followed, or did you notice anything out of the ordinary leading up to the attack?"

"No, nothing like that, but we weren't exactly friends. We just worked together." Chloe shook her head as the past threatened to collide with the present. She'd answered all these questions for the detectives who'd worked her case. "We'd go out to drinks with some of the other doctors on my team every once in a while to celebrate a successful week. The last time had been a couple weeks before Roberta disappeared. We were supposed to meet up again at our regular bar, all of us, but…"

His attention pressurized the air in her lungs. "But what?"

Tension teased the space between her eyebrows, and a rush of exhaustion slithered through her. She swept her tongue across suddenly dry lips. "We— my team and I—lost a patient after a routine mitral valve repair procedure. We were treating her for stenosis, which is a narrowing in the inflow valve of the heart. Everything went according to plan, but a few days after the surgery, the patient's discomfort was out of control. Not even morphine dulled her discomfort. I…I wanted to submit her to an angiogram and see what was causing her so much pain, but before I had the authorization, she died of cardiac arrest. It didn't make sense. She was a healthy woman in her thirties. Nothing about her medical history or health told me she wouldn't come out on the other side of surgery. Turns out, my instincts were right."

"What do you mean?" Weston asked.

"Her family didn't want an autopsy done. Her husband was grieving. He was in shock. He just wanted her buried so he and their children could move on with their lives, but I couldn't get her off my mind." Sweat trickled in a line down her back. "Before the clinic released her remains, I performed my own autopsy against the family's wishes. I found a clamp still in her chest, one we'd missed before suturing her up after the surgery was completed.

It's never happened before, and I don't know how I missed it. The day I was attacked, I was going to inform the board of the mistake."

A striking of a loud cattle bell broke through the comfortable silence between them, and the present ripped her from the past.

"Lunch is ready." Weston cleared his throat before striding toward the door, collecting the photo of him and his wife from the table along the way. He reached for the old dented brass knob, hesitation clear in his rugged features. He twisted the knob and wrenched open the cabin's front door. "Did the patient's husband know the real reason his wife had died?"

Chloe couldn't hug herself any tighter. She shook her head. "No. Nobody knew. As soon as I saw the clamp in her chest, I panicked. I should've left it in as proof, but the more I ran through the procedure, the surer I was I hadn't been the one to leave it behind, that one of the other doctors on my team had. I removed it and stitched her back up so she could be released to her family."

"Where is it now?" he asked.

"Someplace safe." She couldn't tell him any more than that. Not without putting him in more danger than he already was. If the killer was tying up loose ends by coming after her and Roberta Ellis, there was a chance he'd turn his sights to Weston. Too many people had been hurt already.

"You and your team might've lost your medical licenses if you'd gotten the chance to tell the board what went wrong." The slight change in his expression said he was putting together the pieces, the ones she'd tried denying all these months. "How many other physicians were in the surgical suite with you that day?"

Her breath shuddered out of her chest. She'd known this day would come, when she'd have to face the truth, when hiding wouldn't be enough to keep her safe. "Apart from me and Roberta, three other doctors. The resident surgeon who assisted me, a scrub tech and a nurse."

Weston replaced his hat on his head. "Then that's where we start."

THREE SUSPECTS. Three potential killers.

After lunch, Weston filled out the incident report for the crime scene in Contention Mine from one of the other satellite cabins on the property. One void of memories. It was the same set up here as Chloe's and Easton's quarters, only this one had been decorated with soft flannels and darker woods. Perfect for tourists looking to experience the outdoors without leaving some comforts behind.

The end of his pen tapped against the glass of the frame Chloe had recovered from the kitchen drawer, and a knot of guilt set up residence in his gut. The photo had been taken before he and Cynthia had gotten married, the years of their on-again/ off-again relationship barely evident in their smiles. He hadn't talked to anyone about his wife's diagnosis or her passing, not in years. But for some reason he'd found talking to Chloe comforting. Easy, even. There hadn't been an ounce of pity in her expression, no apologies for his loss, as if she knew expressions of condolence sometimes meant more to the giver than to the recipient. Just a simple understanding between them. They'd both lost people they cared about to unpreventable circumstances, but she stood there as a testament for life after loss. Strong, realistic, beautiful.

The past day had threatened to rip him and this town apart, but with her personal insight into the investigation, they actually had a chance of solving the case. He might not have any other deputies to share the weight of protecting Battle Mountain, but he had Chloe, which was more than he could ask for.

A flash of wide pale green eyes and a quick full smile filled his head in an instant, and his heart rate ticked up a notch. His scalp prickled as the nerve endings in his hand woke with remembered warmth when he'd tackled her to the floor inside of Jacob Family Funeral Home. Hints of her perfume still clung to his coat, but it was the feel of her pressed against him that'd engrained itself in his brain.

Weston forced himself to focus on the paperwork in front of him, and not on the kernel of attraction for the newest resident in town. He'd lost Cynthia to circumstances he couldn't prevent. His vow to protect her, to cherish and love her—it'd been everything to him, but it hadn't been enough to save her. Becoming police chief of this town was the only thing that'd saved him from locking himself behind one of these cabin doors and hiding from the world like his brother. Connections like the one stringing between him and Chloe led to emotions. Emotions led to vulnerability. He couldn't go through that kind of loss again. Wouldn't.

Weston finished filling out the incident report from Whitney Avgerpoulos's death scene and moved on to the paperwork for the shooting that'd occurred this morning. Lunch had been a rushed affair once his parents had started their interrogation, but Chloe had handled each and every question with humor and interest. In that short time, it'd been all too easy to imagine the coroner visiting his parents for future lunches, happily chatting with them when they came into town, getting to know every aspect of his family. As though she belonged. It'd been then the barrier he'd relied on against the grief determined to shred him from the inside seemed to crack. Because of her easy-going nature, her laugh, her sincerity. Because of her.

But as much as he'd wanted to pretend reality didn't apply out here at the ranch as he had so many times before, a killer had followed Chloe to Battle

Mountain. Five physicians had been involved in the wrongful death of one of Chloe's patients. One had already been murdered with the same MO as Whitney Avgerpoulos. Roberta Ellis, the anesthesiologist. He was running gun ownership records on the others but doubted there'd be a hit. Whoever'd killed Whitney had gone as far as wiping down the refrigerator used to suffocate and bury her with a cleaning solution that smelled of bleach. Someone who took that much care not to leave behind DNA evidence wouldn't willingly register a weapon they'd planned on using for another attempt. But why the change in MO? Why try to bury Chloe three months ago, succeed with Whitney, then attack a second time with a gun? It didn't make sense.

His phone pinged with an incoming email. The background checks he'd requested for each doctor, including Chloe, filled the screen. No registered weapons, which meant the shooter had either purchased the weapon illegally or stolen the gun to do the job. No outstanding warrants, arrest records or parking tickets, either. The staff who assisted Chloe that day in surgery were clean. "Damn it."

Why else would Chloe and the anesthesiologist have been targeted if not for what happened during that patient's surgery? And what did that have to do with Whitney Avgerpoulos's death?

Weston sent an email to Denver PD's chief of police. Despite the lack of resources and support for po-

lice investigations in Battle Mountain, it'd been easy
to request a warrant for all three suspects' records.
Especially when granted by the only judge in town.

According to the background information he'd
gathered on all five surgical team members, each
lived within Denver's city limits up until Chloe fled
three months ago. The resident surgeon who assisted
Chloe during the surgery, Michael Kerr, had graduated at the top of his class from University of North
Carolina–Chapel Hill, the best medical school in the
country, in primary care before joining the staff at
the heart and vascular center last year. His last name
alone raised the hairs on the back of Weston's neck,
and a cursory study of the man's lineage confirmed
his instinct. Michael Kerr was the son of Senator
Miranda Kerr out of Ohio, but that didn't mean he
wasn't capable of murder. Being in the political spot-
light from the time he'd been born was sure to have
added pressure to succeed.

Luke McMillan, the scrub tech, had been working
at the clinic for six years, never once having been
promoted or awarded a raise in that time according
to his financial records. No debt to speak of aside
from the man's home and no large payments incoming or outgoing to suggest illicit activities. Married with two children with his salary as the single
source of income. A mistake like the one Chloe had
described could be the trigger to make a man like
McMillan desperate to protect his family.

And Celeste Stanley, the nurse assigned to assist that day, still had over fifty thousand dollars in student loan debt to contend with for the next decade. Single, a fierce dog lover according to her social media accounts and an advocate for breaking down complicated medical practices and terminology for her masses of followers. From the collection of comments across her posts and the photos tagged by friends and family, she was generally well liked and the life of the party. No evidence of a connection to the patient who'd died from the clamp in her chest or anything other than a professional relationship with the physicians she worked with, but the records, the social media accounts, the background check—none of them went back further than four years ago, which meant Celeste had changed her name. Why? Then again, Chloe distinctly remembered a male attacker, which could take Celeste out of the running.

Weston made a note to check public records before reviewing the shift schedules Chloe had given him access to through the clinic's employee portal. All five team members had operated together on half a dozen occasions over the years, but there were no other reports of malpractice or problems between doctors. At least not as far as he could tell. Chloe and Roberta Ellis only had one thing in common: they'd both been attacked by the same killer.

He moved onto the next background check and

sat a bit straighter in his seat. Dr. Chloe Miles had been born in Denver, excelled through high school and had graduated from Harvard Medical School before completing her residency at Mount Sinai in New York City. She'd immediately returned to Colorado and taken up the head surgical position at the heart and vascular center, and a ping of understanding hit. Even with the world at her feet and a far brighter future ahead of her, she'd come home.

All three suspects had motive for wanting to stave off a malpractice suit. He just had to find the right one capable of murder. A gust of wind shifted the trees through the side window and rattled the screen. There was one other possibility, one that had nothing to do with the motives of the physicians who'd been in that surgical suite, and everything to do with the patient who'd died at the hands of one of her doctors.

He scanned through Chloe's schedule. She hadn't given him the patient's name, but he knew from talking with her the surgery had to have occurred a couple months prior to her police report. The months scrolled by until he landed on her calendar for that month. Whoever'd organized her calendar had done so by type of appointment and color-coded surgeries red to stand out from the rest of her appointments. There. Only three surgeries the entire month. Logging into the government's public access for lawsuits and court filings, Weston searched by Chloe's name. The results narrowed down to one. "Bingo."

Three light knocks penetrated through the haze he'd lost himself in for the past two hours. He shoved to his feet, his own footsteps overly loud in his ears, and wrenched open the door. An automatic smile turned up one corner of his mouth as Chloe centered herself in the door frame, and a lightness filled him that hadn't been there a minute ago. He hiked a thumb over his shoulder. Nervous energy skittered down his spine as he considered the information he'd uncovered. "Hey, I was just finishing up the paperwork from the shooting this morning. Everything okay?"

"Yeah. I couldn't sleep. I kept thinking about your mom's corn chowder and how I might be able to sneak back into the main house for more without being caught." Chloe raised her shoulders to block the wind ripping through the trees and sweeping her hair into her face. "Any luck on narrowing down a suspect?"

"Yeah. Why don't you come inside? Storm's going to be here soon." Weston reached out, curling one hand around her wrist wrapped securely against her chest, and helped her over the threshold. He secured the door behind him and shut out the cold. He rounded the small kitchen table and stared down at the court-issued paperwork filling the screen. "I've gone through financials and background checks on each of the physicians who were there with you during the surgery. Without interviewing them myself, there's not much to work on, but I can think of one person who might want to kill you and anyone else who was in that surgical suite that day." He spun the laptop toward her. "The patient's husband was suing you for the wrongful death of his wife."

Chapter Six

She couldn't think, couldn't breathe.

She'd been so tied to the idea her admission of malpractice had been the catalyst for getting Roberta Ellis and Whitney Avgerpoulos killed, she'd blinded herself to the motive right in front of her. "Jonathan Byrd is…suing me?"

Blood drained from her face and pooled in the throbbing recesses behind her ears. No. That wasn't possible.

"You didn't know?" The bite left Weston's voice, and the tension between his neck and broad shoulders drained. The fine lines around his eyes deepened, and suddenly he looked much older than midthirties. Raw, even. The past day had added a weight she'd never meant for him to shoulder. Clouds darkened the ridge protecting the Whispering Pines Ranch and cast a wide shadow across his exhausted features. He'd been running off adrenaline and little rest since he'd called her to that mine late last night.

They both had. Weston bent to read through whatever he'd meant to show her on his laptop screen. Court documents? "The lawsuit was filed a week before your attack. Is it possible he learned of the mistake your surgical team made and tried to take things into his own hands instead of waiting for the courts?"

"You think he's the one who attacked me and Roberta, who followed me here and killed Whitney Avgerpoulos?" Chloe unclenched her fists and forced her knees to hold her upright. Confusion and desperation combined into a violent quake of emotion. She shook her head. "No. I know Jonathan Byrd. I talked to him for hours during the months leading up to his wife's surgery. He works as a handyman and likes to go to the movies on the weekends. He was grateful we were able to help his family. He wouldn't hurt anyone, least of all the physicians who saved her life."

"Even if he learned your team was the reason she died?" Weston's expression softened as he closed the distance between them, slowly, as though approaching a wild animal. "Grief changes people. Think about it, Chloe. Out of everyone who was in that surgical suite, out of everyone who had something to lose when your patient died, Jonathan Byrd lost the most. He lost the one person he counted on being with him for the rest of his life."

He was speaking from experience. She knew that,

and logically his theory made sense, but her brain refused to superimpose Jonathan Byrd's face where the black ski mask silhouette haunted her dreams. Refused to acknowledge he would go out of his way to harm an innocent young woman who had nothing to do with his wife's death.

"Handymen have easy access to old refrigerators," he said. "You have to admit, he's worth looking into, even if it turns out we're wrong."

He was right. She knew that. She slid her hands into her coat, frostier than she'd been outside. "For not ever working a homicide investigation before, you sure seem to know what you're doing."

"I'm a fast learner," he said. "Besides, I'm just doing my job."

"It's more than that. You care about this town. You'll do whatever it takes to keep it safe." She shifted her weight to the back of her heels. So much violence, so much blood. When would it end? With her death? With Weston's? The thought of finding another body, of watching the police chief—the man in front of her—or his family pay the price for her mistake, churned a wall of nausea in her stomach. She hadn't been in Battle Mountain long, but the detachment she'd held on to these past couple of months had thinned in that time. In the way Reagan remembered her coffee order at Caffeine and Carbs, how Mr. Jacob invited her to accompany him and his son to lunch every day to make sure she got something to eat, how Weston had stopped her on the street to see how she was adjusting to small-town life. Even the way James and Karie Ford had instantly welcomed her into their lives with the offer of a place to sleep and a hot meal. Everything about this town had worked under her skin, become part of her. Despite her determination to keep her distance from the people here, she'd come to know and appreciate every single one of them. "Maybe that's why I should leave."

She hadn't meant for the words to slip, but she couldn't take them back. A vise squeezed around her heart as deep brown eyes locked on her.

"I feel like we've already had this conversation when you snuck out my parents' bathroom window." Weston stood a bit taller, every ounce the hardworking police chief she'd come to admire. Committed, reliable, loyal—everything she hadn't realized she'd miss when she left her career, her friends and her life behind in Denver. "We agreed we have a higher chance of solving this case together."

Chloe fixated on the framed photo she'd discovered during her cursory search of her cabin, the same cabin Weston and his wife had occupied up until her death nearly four years ago. He'd already lost the most important person in his life. She couldn't be the one to cause him more pain. "Every minute I'm here is another chance someone I care about gets hurt, and I won't be able to live with myself if that person is you. I appreciate everything you've done for me, but I can't risk your life like that. Not when there's something I can do to protect you and this town."

"Whether or not my life is at risk during this investigation isn't up to you." Weston gently framed her jaw with the palm of his hand, forcing her to look up at him. A shot of warmth penetrated through the layer of ice that'd cut her off from feeling anything but fear these past few months. "I made the choice to put my life on the line when I became this town's police chief, Chloe. I knew the risk and so does my family, and I was willing to do this job anyway. And having you here… You're an integral part of this case. I need you here."

She'd become a cardiothoracic surgeon to save lives, to be the best option for patients who needed the finest care. She'd gone out of her way to ensure she'd never be put back in the same position she'd been in during her attack. Helpless, incapable, useless, but right then she'd never felt stronger. Weston needed her. Whether he'd meant personally or professionally, she didn't care. A shift rocked through her, and Chloe raised onto her toes.

She pressed her mouth to his.

His lips gave under the pressure a split second before he took control of the kiss, and the numbness drained from her veins. Her pulse ticked hard at the base of her throat as she parted her lips. He fit against her from her shoulders to her knees, and she swore right then her blood started boiling. A groan escaped up her throat as Weston fisted one hand in her coat collar. Her ears rang, every cell in her body on fire. For him.

He dragged his mouth from hers on a strong gasp. Regret contorted his features into a gut-wrenching mask. "We can't... We can't do this. I'm sorry if I gave you the impression I was interested in more than a professional relationship, but I'm not in a position to commit to anything but my job, Dr. Pascale."

Dr. Pascale.

Her fingers ached to hold on to him, even as he released his grip on her. Chloe cleared her throat as rejection burned through her. She stumbled back, all too aware of the thickening tension between them and the sting of tears forming in her eyes. "Right. No. I understand. I must've... You're right. I misunderstood. I'm sorry, too." She turned toward the door. He'd said he needed her, and something inside had jumped at the opportunity, but she could see now the circumstances that'd brought them together outweighed the kernel of hope in her chest. She should've seen it before now, should've known. Weston Ford could never be hers. Not when a killer had targeted her, and not when he'd gone out of his way to set the photo of him and his wife at his workspace. Eager to put as much distance between them as possible, she wrenched the door open, and a frigid blast of wind slammed into her face. "Do you think you could get ahold of Roberta Ellis's autopsy report? I wanted to run through my notes from Whitney Avgerpoulos's autopsy and compare them with hers. See if they have something in common."

Heavy footsteps closed in from behind. "Chloe, wait—"

A gunshot exploded through the darkening evening.

She automatically hit the floor, hands over her head, but this time there were no screams. No shattering glass. Craning her head up, she searched the limited view of the property framed by the cabin's front door. Her heart threatened to beat out of her chest as she waited for the pain, but it never came. "Weston?"

"I'm fine." Strong hands secured her against his chest as he pulled her out of the doorway and behind the small kitchen cabinet. The police chief shot to his feet and collected his sidearm from the counter. Balanced on both knees, he threaded his arms through the shoulder holster and grabbed for his coat from one of the kitchen chairs. Weston got to a low crouch to peer out the window over the kitchen sink. "That shot came from somewhere close by."

"How can you be sure?" Chloe asked.

"I've been in these woods enough growing up to know where every member of my family was while we hunted game." Hardness entered his expression.

"It could be one of them." She peered around the

corner of the cabinet, meeting only darkness on the other side of the door frame.

"Not this late at night. Family rules. We only hunt in daylight, and we always tell each other when we're headed out." He bent on one knee, leveraging his other leg at a ninety-degree angle. Weston dropped the magazine from his weapon, seemed to count the rounds inside and shoved it back into place. He pulled back on the slide, and the soft click of a round loading into the chamber reached her ears. In less than three breaths, he'd transformed from the guilt-laden man she'd kissed into the police chief determined to protect his town. His gaze cut to hers. "Someone else is out here."

THE STORM HAD ARRIVED.

"Stay here. No matter what happens or what you hear, do not leave this cabin. Understand?" Weston stretched his dominant hand back and pried open the cabinet under the sink. He tore the weapon he'd taped to the underside free. Handing it off to her, he slid his finger alongside her inner wrist. Air caught in his lungs from the small point of contact, but it was nothing compared to the electrifying kiss they'd shared a few minutes ago. He couldn't think about that right now. Whispering Pines had been breached, and he'd do whatever it took to protect his family—to protect her—from the threat. He pulled a flashlight from under the same cabinet. "Safety is here. There are fifteen rounds in the magazine. Don't open this door for anyone until I come back."

Chloe nodded, those brilliant eyes wide. "Be careful. Please."

"You, too." Two simple words, but there was an unspoken weight behind them. In less than a day, she'd triggered his protective instincts and claimed a piece of him. How was that possible? He left the cover of the cabin. Flakes fell in a thin veil as the clouds rolled softly above. Wind kicked up through the trees and mimicked the chaotic storm churning through him. The exposed skin along the backs of his hands and neck burned as he stepped out into the open. The small porch protested under his weight. Snow crunched beneath his boots as he maneuvered into the clearing between the main cabin and the satellite structures around the property.

Muffled footsteps filled his ears from his right, and he raised his weapon, taking aim. Two figures jogged down the main cabin steps. The rack of a shotgun echoed through the night. Instant recognition hardened the muscles down his spine. "Whoever you are, I suggest getting the hell off our property before you have to spend the rest of your short life pulling buckshot from your gut," a familiar voice said.

"Mom, it's me." Weston lowered his sidearm, crossing the clearing. He pressed his back into the main cabin wall, and the outline of both of his parents, each armed, filled in. Their night robes dragged through the flurry of snow settling, their pajama pants tucked into their boots. "You both heard the shot."

"Wasn't us. We made the family rules. We have to stand by them. Lead by example and all that crap." His dad scanned the property with the barrel of the same shotgun he'd taught Weston how to shoot with when he'd only been waist-high, leading the way.

"Thank goodness you're okay." His mother leveraged the shotgun in the crook of her arm and brought him in for a one-armed hug. "Where's Chloe?"

"In my cabin." He pulled back and studied the landscape. "She's armed. I told her to shoot anyone who came through the door, so steer clear."

"Sounded like a semi-auto pistol. Coming from near Easton's cabin." His dad motioned toward the far cabin. "But it couldn't have been your brother."

Easton hadn't picked up a firearm since he'd returned home. They all knew that. Unless his brother had felt threatened.

Panic flooded adrenaline through his veins. A killer had targeted Chloe. If the bastard had come for her... Weston caught sight of the footprints leading away from his brother's cabin. "Go back inside. Lock the doors."

"Like hell we will. Someone comes for one of us, they come for all of us. We'll stay near Chloe." His mother pushed him toward the far cabin. "You find the idiot who dared take on this family."

Weston dashed across the clearing, his boots slipping on the lightweight snow. He tightened his grip around his weapon as he traced the footprints back to their origin. Easton's front door stood slightly ajar. His brother was one of the most security-oriented men he'd ever met. He'd never leave his door unlocked, let alone open. Even out here where the only people he had to worry about were the ones who wouldn't let him disappear into depression and grief. He did a quick check inside. Empty. Outside, Weston rounded to the back, following the tracks there. The footprints disappeared into the tree line, but he'd grown up in these woods. There wasn't a single acre he hadn't memorized over the years.

He ran straight into the darkness.

Ice burned down his throat the harder he pushed himself. Easton was a trained Special Forces Green Beret, but the man who'd murdered Roberta Ellis and Whitney Avgerpoulos—the man who'd tried to kill Chloe—wasn't the kind of killer who'd cease fire upon agreed terms. Weston wasn't going to leave his brother to fight alone. He hit the power button for the flashlight. Pine needles scratched at his neck and face. The snow was falling heavier now. The footprints would be buried under a fresh layer of flakes in a matter of minutes. His breath crystalized in front of his mouth. "Damn it, Easton. Where the hell are you?"

The footprints ended. Impossible. He scanned the area around him, searching for an indication of where his brother had gone, but it was as though Easton had vanished. No sign of a struggle. No evidence his brother had simply turned around and gone back the way he'd come.

A branch snapped off to his left.

Weston dropped the flashlight, spun toward the sound and hiked his pistol shoulder-level. One second. Two. The trees seemed to close in around him. The hairs on the back of his neck stood on end. Wetting his chapped lips, he whistled a short burst of varying notes, the signal he and Easton had used as kids when they'd gotten separated during hunts.

No answer.

Movement registered from behind, and Weston took aim. He hadn't imagined the sound of the gunshot. He hadn't imagined the footprints. Someone was out here, and his brother had noticed. Had Easton broken his own rules to warn him about what was coming? "You're trespassing on private land. Identify yourself."

The trees rustled with another round of movement. Weston held his ground, his weight evenly distributed between both feet, just as his father had taught him. The flashlight reflected back off something within the trees, and just as he fit his finger over the trigger, a ram cleared the tree line. Bleating filled the clearing.

Tension drained from his arms, and he lowered his weapon. "Damn it."

Someone slammed into him from behind.

His gun slipped from his grip and disappeared into the snow and brush a few feet away. Weston hit the ground. Flakes worked under the collar of his jacket as he wrenched one elbow back. He made contact with the assailant's skull. A groan of pain cut through the silence, but his attacker held on. Pain exploded across the side of his head with a right hook to his temple, and white streaks filled his vision.

Weston flipped onto his back and braced against gloved hands wrapping around his neck. A dark ski mask hid his attacker's features, but the weight and shape pinning him to the ground was distinctly male. He widened his arms and dragged the bastard closer. "You picked the wrong family to mess with."

"Who said I'm here for your family?" The man above him countered the leverage Weston had around his wrists, crushing his own hands against Weston's chest. The son of a bitch hauled one fist back and rocketed it into Weston's face. Once. Twice. A third time.

Lightning overwhelmed his senses as his head rammed back into the ground. Darkness closed in around the edges of his vision. *Chloe.* The suspect shoved to his feet, and the pressure against his chest released. "You can't have her."

"You should've stayed out of it, Chief Ford." The man's outline blended in with the trees a split second before the sky tilted on its axis. "Now I'm going to have to hurt you and your brother to make sure you don't interrupt my plans."

His heels dragged into the snow and dirt. Weston clawed at the hand gripped around the back of his coat but couldn't reach. Dizziness arced through him. He tried to reach for the knife he'd secured under his pant leg, but his attacker released his hold before he had the chance. "Where is…Easton? What did you do with him?"

"Don't worry, Chief. You and your brother will have all the time in the world together. Chloe's going to pay for what she's done, and there's nothing you can do to stop me. I'd do you the favor of sedating you, but I only brought enough propofol for one." The man in the mask crouched over him, patting him down for weapons. He pulled the blade from the ankle holster under his pant leg and twisted it back and forth, back and forth. The killer straightened and set one foot against Weston's stomach. "I learned a lot from her escape a few months ago. My main takeaway? Dig the hole first."

A single push. That was all it took, and Weston was falling. Rock, snow and dirt scratched at his face and hands before the ground disappeared out from underneath him. He landed on something soft. His head cleared enough to recognize the familiar scent of bleach just before the lid secured him inside. "No!"

Pitch darkness engulfed him as the reverberation of chains echoed into the box. He pressed both hands against the lid, but the physics of being in such a confined space and the ache in his head stole his strength. His attacker had locked him in a meat freezer. The hard thump of rock and gravel hitting the exterior of the container punctured through the ringing in his ears. The suspect was burying him alive. Weston struck the lid again and pressed his knees into the door as hard as he could. It was no use. It wouldn't budge. "Damn it."

A moan filled the small space. "Language."

"Easton?" He tried to maneuver around to face his brother, but the space was too tight for the both of them to move comfortably. He was positioned directly on top of Easton, their backs pressed against one another.

"Bastard got the drop on me. I think I got a shot off, but my memory is a bit fuzzy after that. You know, from the concussion." Easton shifted beneath him, and his voice became clearer. "I know we're brothers and all, and we used to sleep in the same tent, but could you get your elbow out of my ribs?"

"In case you haven't noticed, we've been locked in a freezer and buried. Would you prefer one of my other body parts instead?" Chloe had been able to calculate how long Whitney Avgerpoulos had between the time the killer had put her in the freezer and the moment she'd taken her last breath. But with two adult men, that time didn't apply. With him and Easton out of commission, the woman he'd given his word to protect was in danger. "We have to work fast. We're about to run out of air."

Chapter Seven

A tremor worked through her despite the warmth from the fireplace.

The snow was falling heavier now and building on the edges of the windowsill. The gun slipped from the sweat building between her palm and the grip as she studied every shift in the trees. Nothing but the wind. Weston had left nearly twenty minutes ago. Where was he? Was he okay?

A knot of concern urged her to check on James and Karie, but leaving the cabin went against everything Weston had instructed. The second she stepped out the front door, she'd be exposed. It was her fault a killer had come to their town. Her fault the man who'd attacked her had killed again. She had a responsibility to make things right, but deeper, the loneliness of the past few months had ebbed the moment the Fords had brought her into their tight-knit fold. She couldn't leave them to pay for her mistakes, and she wouldn't leave Weston to fight her battles alone.

Setting the gun on the kitchen table beside the photo of the police chief and his wife, Chloe tucked her hair into her coat collar and zipped up. She could still taste him on her lips, smell him on her skin. Smoked birch and man mixed with a hint of peppermint. Soothing and exhilarating at the same time. She'd come to Battle Mountain to start over, to never have to face the helplessness she'd felt during her attack. The last thing she'd expected was him. And while Weston had made it perfectly clear he wasn't ready to give up the past, she'd reveled in the feel of someone else fighting to hold her together. That alone was worth the risk. "You can do this."

She collected the gun he'd lent her and clicked off the safety. The weapon was heavy in her hand. Nothing like her surgical tools yet just as deadly. Twisting the old brass knob, she wrenched open the wooden door and stepped out into the open. Winds whipped at her hair as snow melted against her face and neck. She hid in her coat's faux-fur hood, but nothing could cut through the freezing temperatures. Her ears burned with the wind chill as she narrowed her eyes against the onslaught of the storm. Her boots sank into the layer of snow as she headed straight for the main house. A low whistle filled her ears as another gust ripped through the trees. High peaks demanded attention around the property as though a thick layer of black velvet had been draped over them. She couldn't see anything out here, couldn't hear. One hand grasping to keep her hood in place, she picked up the pace toward the dim lights of the main cabin.

Her boots thumped against old wood as she climbed the now-familiar steps leading to the front door. She'd barely lifted her hand to knock before the door swung inward.

"Chloe, what are you doing out here? Weston told us you're supposed to stay in his cabin until he gets back." Karie Ford, armed with one of the largest shotguns Chloe had ever seen, motioned her inside. "Come on, honey. No use in letting you freeze to death. I've got hot chocolate on the stove."

She ducked inside, brushing snow from her coat, and stomped her feet against a smaller version of the handwoven rug she'd noticed in the living room. Chloe pushed her hood back onto her shoulders. "I'm sorry. I just wanted to make sure you and James were okay. It's been almost thirty minutes since Weston left, and the storm is getting worse. You haven't heard from him, have you?"

"No." An internal concern slipped into Karie's brown gaze as the Ford matriarch set her weapon beside the door. "Temperatures are dropping, and he wasn't wearing more than his sheepskin coat, but my boys know these woods better than the backs of their hands. I'm sure they're fine."

"Boys?" Panic squeezed around Chloe's heart. "You mean Easton is out there, too?"

"The shot came from near Easton's cabin. I taught my boys how to track. The snow will complicate things, but they're good hunters. Whoever's out there doesn't stand a chance." James Ford rounded the corner with two steaming white mugs in hand and offered one to her and one to his wife. "Here, drink up. You look like you're about to fall over."

Both of the Ford sons had gone out into the woods in the dead of night in the middle of a snowstorm. Chloe stumbled back toward the door, the gun heavier than a minute ago. "I have to go. I have to find them before it's too late."

"Chloe, Weston would want you to stay here. You're safe with us." Karie handed off her mug back to her husband and countered Chloe's retreat. That sugar-sweet voice that'd greeted her when Weston had introduced her to these people solidified as hard as overcooked caramel. "You don't know the land or how to survive in these conditions. The second you walk out that door, you'll be putting yourself in danger, and my son did not risk his life to protect you for you to do something stupid."

"The man who tried to bury me alive, who killed Whitney Avgerpoulos and one of my colleagues, followed me to Battle Mountain. He won't stop until he gets what he wants." She squared her shoulders, more herself than ever before. "You and your family are the only ones standing between him and me. Whitney had nothing to do with any of this, and he killed her anyway. Do you think he'll spare your sons' lives just because they're not his original target, or do you think he'll eliminate anyone who gets in his way?"

One second. Two. Karie Ford notched her chin higher, but the hardness drained from her expression. "Honey, Easton is former Special Forces, and Weston has been police chief of this town going on three years. They've trained with weapons. What do you think you can do to stop whoever is after you that they can't?"

"I don't know, but I'm not going to be the reason you lose your sons tonight. I'm going after them, and there's nothing you can do to stop me." Chloe handed off the mug of hot chocolate and escaped out the front door, immediately tensing at the wall of cold seeping past layers and straight into bone.

"You're not going alone, kid." James Ford closed the front door behind him and secured a thick winter hat over his gray hair. With a rifle slung across his back, he slid gloves onto each hand and tossed a similar set of gloves and a matching hat to her. "Here, put these on. You're going to need 'em."

Hesitation crushed her from the inside, but she wouldn't deny she had no idea where she was going or how to track Weston's and Easton's movements. James had said it himself. He'd trained his boys. Who better to help her find them than the expert? Chloe leveraged the gun between her thighs as she donned the winter gear, but James was already on the move and walking around the back of the cabin. "You said Weston headed behind Easton's cabin. Where are you going?"

"Storm's getting worse. We need to move fast before the snow covers their tracks." He stopped in front of a garage and hefted the heavy door above his head. Inside, he stepped between two identical four-wheelers most likely used to tend the land. Throwing one leg over the machine, he twisted the key in the ignition, and the ATV growled to life. James hiked his thumb over his shoulder and reached back for a helmet. "Climb on."

She approached from the opposite side and ma-neuvered into position behind him. The machine vibrated beneath her as she clipped the straps of the helmet securely around her chin. Chloe clicked the safety on the weapon Weston had lent her and slid it into her pocket. She'd never ridden an ATV or a motorcycle before, and the fear of sliding off the back stuck in her throat. The chemical burn of gasoline and exhaust filled her lungs. "I don't know what I'm supposed to do."

James craned his chin over his shoulder, his voice barely breaking through the growl of the engine and the padding around her ears. "Put your arms around me, and hang on."

The all-terrain vehicle jolted forward, and Chloe held on for dear life. The garage disappeared behind them as they rocketed through the snow, the change of gears loud in her ears. Her heart rate shot into her throat as they raced across the property directly toward Easton's cabin. Snow liquefied against the helmet's visor, cutting off her view, but James seemed to know exactly which direction his sons had gone. Pine branches laden with at least two inches of snow blurred in her vision the faster Weston's father pushed the four-wheeler, but in an instant, momentum threw her forward as he downshifted.

They slowed to a stop, and James pointed to their right. Darkness fled at the spread of the machine's headlights to where she could almost make out dips in the snow alongside them. "Those are Weston's prints. Size ten. These other ones are Easton's. Size eleven. They headed this way."

James knew his sons' shoe sizes. Of course, he did. The ATV launched forward to the compression of the gas before she could respond, her hot breath building in the helmet. The curves of the rifle strapped to James's back bit into her arms, but she didn't dare release her grip or move in any way for fear of disturbing the delicate balance of the machine beneath her.

Pine trees thinned ahead before opening into a wide spread of clearing, and James slowed once again. A loud click notched her heart rate into her throat. The engine died as the Ford patriarch dismounted easily and rounded to the front of the ATV. He crouched, sliding gloved fingers through the snow before studying the landscape around them.

"What is it?" Chloe asked.

"Easton's tracks end, but Weston's…" He pointed off to his left. "There's another set of footprints I don't recognize, heading south. There's a small ravine where an old creek used to cut through our property. It dried up a long time ago, but that's where these tracks lead. Along with a set of drag marks."

Drag marks? Every muscle down her spine tensed. The third set of tracks headed toward the creek. Not Weston's or Easton's. "You think—"

The growl of another engine cut through the soft ringing in her ears.

James pushed to his feet, twisting around a split second before a second set of headlights illuminated the clearing from a break in the trees.

Chloe shielded her eyes against the sudden brightness but couldn't make out the driver.

A soft clink of chains reached her ears as the truck rocketed toward them.

"Chloe, get out of here!" James stepped between her and the oncoming pickup and shoved her off the four-wheeler.

She hit the ground just as the scream of metal and glass exploded around her. "No!"

THE AIR HAD already thinned.

Weston gasped through the pressure building in his chest, but it was only a matter of time before their bodies exchanged what was left of the oxygen for carbon dioxide. No light. No way out. He pressed his elbow into Easton's chest to reach his cell phone, but his brother's groan told him to back off. "We have to get out of here. Can you reach my phone in my back pocket?"

"I can't reach anything with you on top of me, genius." The words growled from between Easton's teeth as his brother shifted beneath him. "Great plan, luring a killer straight to our property, by the way. You're doing a bang-up job, Chief."

"I asked for your help. You slammed the door in my face." Irritation burned through him, and Weston threw his elbow back into his brother's chest without guilt. Instead, his elbow hit the side wall of the freezer and shot nerve-numbing agony through his forearm and into his fingers. "Fine. I'll do it myself, just like I've done everything else since you came home and started feeling sorry for yourself."

He'd taken an oath to protect the people of Battle Mountain, promised to protect Chloe. Being buried in a freezer wasn't going to stop him and neither was Easton's self-pity. He craned his hand back behind him, joints screaming for relief as he skimmed the top of his jeans pocket with his middle finger. There was no way he could reach it. Not without more room to maneuver or Easton's help, and the wretch obviously wasn't in the mood to help anyone. Let alone himself. Weston slumped back onto his brother. They weren't going anywhere.

"Is that what you think I'm doing?" Easton asked. "Feeling sorry for myself?"

"Honestly, I don't know what you're doing." Weston set both palms straight ahead of him, but he couldn't get the leverage he needed to increase the pressure on the freezer door. Not as long as Easton took up more than half the space. He slid his palms down the length of the container. "All I know is you were my brother when you left on orders. Now you're a stranger. You hide in your cabin, you alienate the people who care about you and you shut us out when we try to help, but damn it, Easton, enough. I need your help to get out of here so I can stop a killer from getting to Chloe. It's time to think about someone else for a change."

The sound of their shallow breathing filled the space. Seconds distorted into minutes. He wasn't sure how long the silence stretched yet felt the weight of time slipping.

Exhaustion urged him to close his eyes, but drifting off, pretending they weren't going to die, would be too easy. Sweat beaded in his hairline, and a deep-rooted fear took control. Losing Cynthia had changed him. In an instant, he'd had everything he'd wanted out of life. A wife, a promising future at another mine up north. And it'd all slipped through his fingers the moment she was diagnosed. He watched her suffer, was there when the life drained from her gaze, and then he was alone. His parents had done what they could to be there for him, but it hadn't been the same, trusting himself completely to another person, of having that person trust him completely. He'd loved his wife, and it hadn't been enough.

How the hell was he supposed to protect Chloe when he couldn't even protect himself? Weston pressed one hand into the side of the freezer to feel for the size of the space.

Damn it. Harshness bled from his voice. "I'm sorry, Easton. I didn't mean… I have no room to talk. I lost Cynthia. I can only imagine how hard it must've been to watch your entire unit die right in front of you and not be able to do a damn thing about it." Weston let his body sink into the confines of the container, and the past rushed to meet the present. "When she died, I was a mess. I couldn't eat, couldn't sleep. I didn't want to talk to anyone or leave my cabin, either. Most of the time, I didn't even know what day it was or how long she'd been gone. Some days were better than others, but honestly, the only thing that helped me move on was becoming police chief of this town. It gave me a reason to get up in the morning, a purpose. That's all I want for you. You battled to save thousands of strangers in the Middle East, and now I'm asking you to help me save one more. Please, don't give up. I can't do this without you."

The tick of his brother's swallow reached his ears.

"Seven months, one week and two days." Easton's voice broke through the darkness. "That's when our convoy was hit by an IED. I lost everyone, and I don't go a single day without remembering their names or what they looked like when I pulled them from the wreckage. I was the only one who survived. A piece of shrapnel penetrated my helmet, but I remember every second of that day, Weston. You managed to pick yourself up and find something you believe in, but I'm not you. You're stronger. You always have been. Over there, I knew the things I was doing made a difference. Here, I'm nothing."

"You're my brother," Weston said, whispering so as not to use up too much air. "That's not nothing. All I ever wanted to be growing up was you. You went into the military and suddenly became this hero Mom and Dad were so proud of. All I ever managed was to stay alive down there in the mine. You…you were everything to me. You still are, and I don't want to lose you again."

His heart rate ticked off the seconds, the minutes.

"Forget the phone. You're not going to get coverage with this storm. Move to your left," Easton said.

Muscled arms reached past him as Weston followed orders, and his body sank into the space between the freezer wall and his brother's side. On level ground, he had room to straighten his arms out in front of him, and he set his hands against the door. "The bastard padlocked us in and buried us under at least a few inches of dirt."

"It's worth a shot. On my count." Easton shifted beside him, their arms brushing against one another. "One, two...three!"

Every muscle he owned protested under the pressure, and pain scorched down his side and into the back of his neck. The door lifted slightly, and a wall of dirt cascaded down into the freezer. It peppered across his face and penetrated the seam of his mouth. Weston shook his head to dislodge it, and a wave of dizziness slithered through him. Time was running out. His arms gave out, and the door thumped back into place. They were burning through the last of the oxygen. "It moved...but the padlock...is still in place."

"We have to keep...trying. Use...legs," Easton said. "No time...for caution."

They could do this. They had to do this. There were no other options. Weston braced his feet against the lower half of the freezer door. "One, two, three."

He used every last ounce of strength he had left. Another wave of dirt fell into the container, half burying him, but he couldn't stop. Not yet. A groan filled the small space before a loud snap. The weight of the door disappeared, and frigid air dove into his lungs. A humorless laugh of relief escaped up his throat, but there was only a minimal amount of space to escape. Gasping for breath, he caught sight of storm clouds above. Bites of snow blew into the freezer and melted against his face. "We did it."

Easton pressed his back into the freezer door, giving Weston a chance to get to his knees. He swept his arm through the ten-inch opening and dislodged some of the dirt wall that'd held them prisoner. "The chains and padlock are still in place. We must've just broken the door handle, but it's enough. We can climb through here. You first."

Weston stretched one hand through the opening and hauled his body through. Turning back, he held the freezer door open as wide as he could as his brother followed behind. He hadn't heard a vehicle engine. The son of a bitch who'd attacked them could still be near. He helped Easton to his feet and released his hold on the door. "He couldn't have gotten far."

"You see that?" Easton asked.

Two beams of light penetrated through the trees to the north. A vehicle? A chemical burn replaced fresh air in his throat, familiar and nauseating. "Smells like one of the four-wheelers, but those lights are too tall to be from one of ours."

"Stay low, move fast. Use me as a shield if you have to." Easton used the trees as cover, Weston on his heels. They'd hunted together for years, shared an awareness of the other as though they were twins.

"You know I'm the older brother, right? I taught you how to hunt. I should be the one telling you to stay low and move fast." Weston pulled up short as they reached the trees and took cover behind one of the larger pines. The snow had lightened, and outlines materialized about twenty feet ahead. "That's a truck."

"And a four-wheeler. One of ours from the look of it." The weight of Easton's attention settled along one side of his face. His voice dipped an octave. "It's been totaled."

Weston scanned the area. No sign of movement or an ambush, but he hadn't seen his attacker until it'd been too late. His instincts prickled, and he stepped free from cover. Something wasn't right. He'd instructed Chloe and his parents to stay inside the cabin. What was one of their ATVs doing out here? His gut knotted as he approached the wreckage, and a familiar outline took shape draped over the front of the machine. Recognition flared. "Dad!"

His heart shot into his throat. He sprinted for his father. His boots slid across the layer of ice under pristine powder, and he went down. Scrambling to his feet, he ignored the bite of frost on his hands as he clamped onto one of the twisted handholds. James Ford lay motionless over the four-wheeler, pinned between the pickup and the ATV. His hands shook as he hesitated moving the older man, and Easton stepped into his peripheral vision. "It's going to be okay. We'll get you out of here." He reached for his phone in his back pocket but came up empty. They were at least a mile from the house. By the time the storm passed, it could be too late.

"Go." The single word punctured through the grief threatening to tear him apart. Blood trickled from his father's mouth, and there was nothing Weston could do to stop it. "Find…her."

"We're not going anywhere. We're going to get you out of here, okay? Hang on, Dad." A vise constricted around his heart and squeezed the air from his chest as though he were right there at Cynthia's bedside all over again. Weston stumbled back. Sorrow lodged in his throat, tears burning against his face. There was so much blood. "Just hang on. Okay? We're going to get you help."

"He took…Chloe. Go." James Ford relaxed against the mangled parts of his four-wheeler. A single exhale escaped past his lips, and then he was gone.

Chapter Eight

A shiver rippled through her.

Wind whistled low from between the slats of the abandoned structure, freezing her jeans solid against her legs. Dropping temperatures kept her from losing consciousness for the time being, but it was only a matter of time before her organs started shutting down to conserve energy. As long as she kept shivering, she had time. She twisted at the bungee cord tightly secured around her wrists. The last images of James Ford flashed across her mind, playing in slow motion. Another torrent of guilt and sadness thickened the sob in her throat. He'd put himself between her and the oncoming truck. He'd saved her life but ended up paying the price. This. This was what she'd been trying to avoid when Weston had brought her to Whispering Pines Ranch. The loss. The pain. The fear. A fresh cut twisted through her heart at the imagery of Weston learning of his father's death. He would blame her. He would hate her. He'd never forgive her.

Chloe dug her heels into the old planks of wood to get her bearings through one of the small windows above her head, but her body protested even the small movements. The man who'd dragged her through the woods—away from the crash—obviously knew this property better than she did. She struggled to get her eyeline above the bottom of the window at her back, but there was only darkness. Her captor had dropped her on the floor and left, but her instincts warned her he hadn't gone far. Was he waiting for her to try to escape? Finishing off Weston and his brother?

The small structure she'd memorized over the past few minutes creaked and groaned under the violence of the storm. No more than five feet by five feet, dark, isolated. A single wooden chair sat in one corner. An old hunting shed? A hunting shed with a crawl space? Another groan of wood shrieked over the constant drone of wind. She listened for crunching snow, footsteps—anything that would give her an idea of where her abductor had gone. There was only the storm. The muscles in her abdomen burned as she brought her heels in closer to her body. Her fingers ached as she skimmed the bungie cord cutting off circulation to her ankles and hands. "Come on."

Chloe tried to work her fingers under the bonds again. Her eyes sagged closed, the corners of the shed blurring at the edges of her vision. She had to stay awake, had to keep trying. Weston and Easton had gone into the woods to find her. Were they still out there? Were they safe? Her fingers curled into her palms against her brain's commands. Exhaustion increased the heaviness in her muscles. She could do this. She had to do this. The pulse behind her ears lightened, her exhales crystalizing in front of her mouth. The temperature had dropped well below freezing. Even with her winter coat and the hat James had lent her, she couldn't last much longer in these conditions. Not without a heat source.

There were five stages to hypothermia. From the quick inventory of her body, she surmised she'd already entered stage one. Shivering, temperature around thirty-three degrees. Stage two would complicate things. The tips of her fingernails had turned blue. From the cold or from lack of blood, she couldn't be sure right then. Didn't matter. "Just keep shivering."

The single door to the shed slammed against the outside wall, and a broad outline filled the door frame. A lantern highlighted dark pants, a heavy jacket, hiking boots. Her automated reflexes froze instead of firing, and she forced her hands away from her ankle binds. Recognition connected memories of her attack three months ago with the man closing the door behind him. Same shape, same build, same black ski mask. "You."

"Me." He secured the door, then turned to face her, removing his gloves in the process. "I've been looking for you, Dr. Miles. Thought I'd caught up with you a couple months ago in Vail, but just as I underestimated you in Denver, you'd already moved on. Here, to Battle Mountain."

The hard thump between her ears, combined with the effects of hypothermia, distorted her abductor's voice. Gravity pulled her upper body to the right, but she caught herself before collapsing to the floor. One of the planks near her feet wobbled under the pressure of keeping herself upright. "Why are you doing this? Why did you have to kill Whitney and James?"

"You dragged that old man into this the moment you accepted his help, Chloe. Just as you dragged the police chief and his brother into this. I'm not sure how else to make it clear to you. Nothing is going to stop me from making sure you pay for what you've done." The killer's footsteps reverberated through the uneven floor as he crossed the small space and dragged the chair into the center of the floor. Directly in front of her. He set an old oil lantern between them. "As for Whitney, well, she was simply in the wrong place at the wrong time. You see, I've spent the past three months hunting you down. I contacted your friends, your family, your coworkers. I even filed a missing person's report on your behalf, but the police had nothing."

He leaned forward, setting his elbows against his

knees, and she caught sight of the streak of dirt along the outer edges of his gloves. "Then it occurred to me you'd actually left Denver. So I started branching out to smaller towns where no one would think to look for you. It turns out you make one hell of an impression on the people you talk to, just as you'd made an impression on me. It was only a matter of time before I caught up with you, but when I learned where you were staying and tried to break in to leave you a little gift, Whitney did what any concerned citizen would do. She confronted me. Unfortunately for her, it was her last good deed. I couldn't have her ruining my surprise. Turns out, she was better than the gift I'd chosen for you anyway."

"She had nothing to do with this. She had an entire future ahead of her." Tears burned in her eyes as pieces of the puzzle settled into place, but three words stood out among the many. The police chief. She'd stopped shivering. Numbness climbed up her arms, past her ankles, but Chloe wasn't going to let him get away with this. No matter what happened, she'd make sure Whitney Avgerpoulos's parents learned of their daughter's bravery. "Why are you doing this? Why kill Roberta Ellis? Why try to kill me?"

A low laugh filled the shed as her abductor shoved to his feet. He closed the distance between them and crouched. His joints popped as he reached for the ski mask and pulled it from his head. Strikingly blond hair turned golden under the warmth of the lantern. Sharp features hazed as he turned an iced expression on her, but she could never forget his face. Thin lips rolled between the killer's teeth as he tossed the mask to the other side of the shed. He'd aged significantly in the past few months since she'd seen him. Where he'd greeted her on more than a dozen occasions with a quick smile and a softness, a hollowness had taken hold, and her heart plummeted in her chest. "Isn't it obvious, Dr. Miles? You killed my wife."

"Jonathan." His name left her mouth through her locked jaw, and she was forced to set her head back against the shed wall. "You're…doing this because of her. You blame me for…what happened."

"Shouldn't I? You promised me my wife's surgery was routine, that the chances of her surviving were over ninety percent." Jonathan Byrd reached behind him, pulling something solid and distinct from his back waistband. A gun. He pointed the barrel at her. Not just any gun. The one Weston had given her before he'd left the cabin. "Turns out she did survive the surgery. What killed her was the clamp you left in her chest."

Chloe struggled to shake her head. Her tongue caught between her lips, rough and dry. How had he found out about the mistake her team had made? She hadn't had the chance to tell the board, and the other physicians wouldn't have willingly put their careers at risk.

"I sat at her bedside every day. I watched her slowly suffocate right in front of me. She was in so much pain not even the morphine could help her at the end. I held her hand until she died, and a piece of me died right along with her." Jonathan straightened, standing over her with the gun gripped in one hand. "I'm going to find the rest of the doctors who were there that day. I'm going to end the lives of each and every single one of them, but today, you're going to know what it feels like to lose someone you care about slowly and painfully."

What? A board shifted under her foot, and Chloe clawed at the bungee cord around her ankles pitifully. It was no use. Her body was already starting to shut down, one organ at a time. She couldn't reach the binds. Not without Jonathan catching her. "I don't…understand."

"I've been watching you, Chloe. I've seen the way you look at him. I see the way you make him smile. You're falling for him." The killer inserted the blade between her ankles and cut through the bungie cord. The strands fell free, and he wrapped his free hand around her arm and hauled her to her feet. "I'd originally brought the freezer out here for you and the police chief, but circumstances have changed. For his brother. Someone will find their bodies in a few days. After I call in an anonymous tip, of course.

There won't be anything you can do about it, but I'll do you a favor. I'll bury you right next to them, and you can take your last breaths together."

Weston. A sob built in her chest but stuck under her sternum as he led her toward the shed door. No. She wrenched out of his hold with everything she had left and knocked the lantern over as she hit the floor. Hot oil spilled across the old wood and caught fire. Chloe stretched both hands out and tried to stand, but her body wouldn't obey her brain's commands. A gust of wind aggravated the fire, and she realized her abductor had vanished. Flames branched from the source and raced up the walls as she clawed toward the door. Instant heat burned the exposed skin of her face and neck as she struggled to shield her eyes against the fire closing in, but it was too late.

There was no escape.

THE SMELL OF burning wood filled his nostrils.

Weston trudged through shin-high powder as he followed the disturbances south across the property. Bare skin burned from exposure, but it wouldn't slow him down. The scent of gasoline still clung to his jacket from the wreckage he'd left behind, the chemical burn thick in his throat. Snow worked into his boots and numbed his fingers. He had to keep going. He needed her to be alive.

He'd left Easton at the crash site. The storm

Treat Yourself with 2 Free Books!

GET UP TO 4 FREE BOOKS & 2 FREE GIFTS WORTH OVER $20

See Inside For Details

Claim Them While You Can

Get ready to relax and indulge with your **FREE BOOKS** and more!

Claim up to FOUR NEW BOOKS & TWO MYSTERY GIFTS – absolutely FREE!

Dear Reader,

We both know life can be difficult at times. That's why it's important to treat yourself so you can relax and recharge once in a while.

And I'd like to help you do this by sending you this amazing offer of up to FOUR brand new full length FREE BOOKS that WE pay for.

This is everything I have ready to send to you right now:

Try **Harlequin® Romantic Suspense** books featuring heart-racing page-turners with unexpected plot twists and irresistible chemistry that will keep you guessing to the very end.

Try **Harlequin Intrigue® Larger-Print** books featuring action-packed stories that will keep you on the edge of your seat. Solve the crime and deliver justice at all costs.

Or **TRY BOTH!**

All we ask in return is that you answer 4 simple questions on the attached Treat Yourself survey. You'll get **Two Free Books** and **Two Mystery Gifts** from each series you try, *altogether worth over $20!* Who could pass up a deal like that?

Sincerely,

Pam Powers

Harlequin Reader Service

Treat Yourself to Free Books and Free Gifts.

Answer 4 fun questions and get rewarded.

▼ DETACH AND MAIL CARD TODAY! ▼

	YES	NO
1. I LOVE reading a good book.	○	○
2. I indulge and "treat" myself often.	○	○
3. I love getting FREE things.	○	○
4. Reading is one of my favorite activities.	○	○

TREAT YOURSELF • Pick your 2 Free Books...

Yes! Please send me my Free Books from each series I select and Free Mystery Gifts. I understand that I am under no obligation to buy anything, as explained on the back of this card.

Which do you prefer?

❏ **Harlequin® Romantic Suspense** 240/340 HDL GRCZ
❏ **Harlequin Intrigue® Larger-Print** 199/399 HDL GRCZ
❏ **Try Both** 240/340 & 199/399 HDL GRDD

FIRST NAME

LAST NAME

ADDRESS

APT.#

CITY

STATE/PROV.

ZIP/POSTAL CODE

EMAIL ❏ Please check this box if you would like to receive newsletters and promotional emails from Harlequin Enterprises ULC and its affiliates. You can unsubscribe anytime.

HI/HRS-520-TY22

made it impossible to get through to the station, but Easton would take care of their father. A swell of grief charged up his throat as the last few moments of James Ford's life played over and over again. His father had been a great man. Strong, loyal, selfless. There wasn't a single moment growing up Weston hadn't been able to count on him, even when the old man had been on military orders.

Tears stung his eyes. Damn it. He couldn't think about that right now. The next step, the next tree. That was all that mattered. The scent of smoke slithered through the pines ahead, and he picked up the pace. The bastard who'd taken Chloe had already killed three people. There was no telling how long she had before she joined that number. "I'm coming, Doc. Just hang on."

As hard as he'd tried to deny the connection building between him and the coroner, he couldn't ignore the panic exploding through his system now. He'd taken an oath to protect her and failed, but it was more than that.

He'd underestimated her determination to defend him and his family, this town even, against her past. He'd underestimated her influence on his thoughts, on his actions and his entire belief system. Her undeniable sense of right and wrong, of making up for the past, had broken through the wall of ice that'd kept him from letting anyone in since his wife's death. He'd never met anyone more committed to the well-being of others, more passionate to set things right than her. She'd made a mistake, resulting in a patient's death, but her sincerity had never been more evident than in the fact she'd convinced his father to join her in the race to find him and Easton.

But, hell, if he were being honest with himself, asking Chloe to see this case through until the end wasn't just about finding Whitney Avgerpoulos's killer. It might've begun that way, but really, he'd started to care about her, and there wasn't anything he wouldn't do to ensure she walked away from this investigation alive.

A waning orange glow pulsed through the trees ahead, and the hairs on the back of his neck stood on end. He slowed as his mind ran through the possibilities, each ending in only one conclusion. Fire. "Chloe."

Weston pushed through a wall of pines cutting him off from a small clearing on the other side. He was familiar with the area, even in the dark, but despite his position as Battle Mountain's police chief, he hadn't been prepared for this fight. Needles and branches sliced across his face and neck. His boots sank into undisturbed snow, slowing him down. Muscles burned with exertion down the front of his thighs. He swung his arms wide to keep momentum, his throat frozen with icy temperatures.

A lick of flame sprinted toward the sky, and he burst into the small clearing where one of their old hunting sheds had caught fire. Instant heat warned him not to get closer, but his instincts said she was here. "Chloe!"

The structure's roof groaned as bits and pieces flaked off and fell around the perimeter of the fire. The shed was going to collapse any second, and every cell in his body said Chloe was inside. Red, orange and yellow embers shot into the air. Nearby young trees smoldered as the flames drew near. Smoke thickened between him and the shed and stung his eyes.

A scream cut through the crackle of flame and cauterized his nerve endings.

"No." Weston sprinted toward what was left of the door, covering his face with both arms. The flames lashed out, and agony shot down his hands and across his face. Weston stumbled back. He couldn't get close enough. Not without some kind of protection. Ripping his coat from his shoulders, he draped it over his head and hands as best he could. Sweat dripped underneath his collar and pooled at the base of his spine. Shifting his weight onto his front leg, he bounced on his back foot and summoned the courage to try again.

Pain splintered across his left shoulder and thrust Weston forward.

He landed palms down into a smoldering pile of wood. His fight-or-flight system twisted him away as fast as his body allowed. He rolled onto his back as a wall of muscle brought down a large branch from above. He threw his forearms out and blocked the blow. An ache ripped through his arms. The attacker pulled back for another strike, and Weston rocketed both feet into the bastard's chest. His coat fell away and exposed more skin to the elements.

He scrambled to his feet. Heat struggled to overcome the stiffness in his bones. He set one foot into the shed. A dark feminine outline—unmoving—was all he recognized before strong hands tore him back. Fire and trees blurred in his vision as he hit the ground a second time. Snow stung down his back and across both arms.

"You just don't quit, do you, Chief?" His attacker closed the distance between them and fisted one hand into Weston's T-shirt. He pulled his free hand back and struck. One hit. Two. "Doesn't matter. I got what I wanted. You're too late. Chloe is going to pay for every single second my wife suffered, and there's nothing you can do about it."

"Over my dead body." Weston dodged the next strike and used the man's own momentum to launch him face-first into the snow. He slammed his elbow into the attacker's back, and a groan drowned out the sound of the crackling flames. He struck again and got to his feet. Hauling his boot into the son of a bitch's rib cage, Weston froze as the killer caught his foot and twisted. His knee planted into the ground and knocked him off balance as lightning arced through his ligaments. He fell forward, palms splayed out in front of him.

"That can be arranged." The killer fisted a handful of hair and forced Weston back onto his knees. The fire lit up sharp angles of the suspect's face and highlighted the curl of a thin mouth. Pain contorted his opponent's expression as his hand trembled against Weston's skull. Jonathan Byrd. The husband of the patient Chloe and her team had lost in the week following her surgery. "I know why you're doing this. I know the pull she has on you and everyone she meets. You think she's innocent, that she deserves your protection, but you're wrong, Chief Ford. She doesn't deserve your loyalty. She'll only use it against you."

The past few weeks flashed through his brain as he recounted his first meeting with Chloe, the way her smile had lit him up from the inside, how she'd gone out of her way to help elderly Mrs. Banes get her groceries to the car. How she'd empathized when he'd told her about Cynthia's diagnosis and death and somehow given him hope for the future in the same breath. No. There wasn't a single part of him that doubted her engrained goodness and honesty.

"I know exactly who she is." Debilitating throbbing gripped his body as Weston forced himself to his feet. The world threatened to rip out from under him, but he powered through. "I know what you're going through. I know how much it hurts to lose the one person you thought you'd be spending the rest of your life with, but you're wrong about Chloe. And there's no way in hell I'm going to let you take her."

He tackled the killer around the middle, and they hit the ground as one. Air crushed from his lungs as they rolled through the snow, each fighting for dominance.

Weston's head snapped back against something harder than ice, and the edges of his vision darkened in waves. A rock? Disorientation cleared enough for him to dodge the next strike aimed at his face, and he wrapped frozen fingers around the rock behind him. Arcing the heavy weapon as fast as he could, he slammed it against the killer's head, and the weight against his chest vanished.

Weston forced himself to sit up and shoved to his feet. He stumbled as dizziness took hold, but he couldn't stop. Couldn't give up. Blocking the heat from his face with both hands, he stepped through the shed's opening. A section of roof crashed to the floor beside Chloe, and he lunged. He gripped both of her ankles and pulled as hard as he could. Her outstretched hands barely cleared the doorway as the structure failed. He landed on his backside a few yards from the shed, and he scrambled to turn her over onto her back. He fought to catch his breath. "I've got you, Doc. It's going to be okay. You're going to make it. Hang on."

He pressed two fingers to the base of her neck.

Her pulse was thready but there, and the battle-ready tension that'd pushed him this far drained. He split his attention from the dark smudges across the underside of her jaw and scanned the area where he and the killer had fought. Weston straightened, keeping one hand pressed to Chloe's neck.

Jonathan Byrd was gone.

For how long, he didn't know. Didn't care. All that mattered was getting Chloe help. He threaded his hands beneath her knees and along her lower back and hefted her against his chest. Every muscle he owned protested the additional weight as he climbed to his feet. He could do this. He had to do this.

Her head sagged against his arm as he retraced his steps through the trees and back toward the wreckage where he'd left Easton and his father. She cracked her eyes open, the distant glow of the fire reflecting back at him. "Bet you wish you'd let me leave now."

Chapter Nine

Her lungs burned.

Smoke inhalation, mild hypothermia, choking grief for someone she'd hardly known. Chloe closed her eyes against the onslaught of noise coming from the monitors tracking her vitals and the afternoon sunlight streaming through the window. Emergency personnel had rushed her to the small medical center located at the southern end of town once they'd been able to get to the main cabin and keep the fire from spreading. The neutral colors eased the headache at the base of her skull, the scratchy sheets long past their prime. What she wouldn't give to be able to go home, to pretend what'd happened out in those woods hadn't been her fault.

Flashes of fear, of pain, exploded through her as she memorized the gauze across her hands concealing the blisters underneath. Jonathan Byrd was systematically and methodically tracking down each surgical team member involved in his wife's death and seeking his own sense of revenge. Roberta Ellis had already paid the price, and he'd come for Chloe twice. It was only a matter of time before the grieving husband set his sights on the others. She'd severed contact with anyone from that life when she'd left Denver, but she wouldn't let anyone else die for a mistake she'd failed to notice during that surgery. No matter who was really at fault. She had to warn them.

Hospital staff had taken her clothes and bagged them as evidence and left a pair of dark blue scrubs as a temporary replacement. Shoving back the blankets, she set her bare feet against the floor and removed the sticky nodes from her skin. The tug of her IV catheter reminded her dehydration had been a large proponent of why she'd gone into hypothermia so quickly, but she couldn't afford to wait around for Jonathan Byrd to strike again. Not when he'd already destroyed so many lives.

She peeled the adhesive sticker from her skin, the sting intensifying at the entry of her IV, and discarded it on the bed. A couple drops of blood backloaded into the line as she pulled the needle from her vein. She stripped the blood pressure cuff from her arm, the Velcro louder than she expected, and stood. Cold worked up through her heels and into bone as she shuffled to the end of the hospital bed. The monitors had gone quiet without anything to report. Dressing quickly, she tossed the thin gown over the blood pressure cuff and slid her legs into the scrub pants. She secured the drawstring and locked her jaw against the ache in her right side from being thrown from James Ford's four-wheeler. She nearly collapsed as she replayed those terrifying seconds over and over. She recalled the acceptance in his eyes as she stared up at him, the gut-wrenching sorrow that'd crushed her as effectively as the pickup slamming into the ATV. Only she'd been the one to walk away.

Chloe forced herself to thread both arms into the scrub top. She shoved her feet into the thin hospital socks with rubber grips on the bottom and realized the nurses had taken her boots along with her clothing.

Three knocks on the door electrified her nerves, and she sat back against the bed.

The mattress creaked under her as Weston filled the doorway, every ounce the police chief she'd needed out there. He'd changed, most likely because he'd surrendered his clothing as evidence as well, but even without the addition of his sheepskin coat, he was still the most rugged, handsome man she'd ever met. He removed his stained hat, circled as far from her as possible and took a seat in the chair a few feet from the bed. Exhaustion had set up in the finer lines of his face and darkened the circles under his eyes. He moved slowly, as though every step triggered another round of pain, and the invisible laceration cutting through her heart carved deeper. He'd been injured out there. Because of her. "Look who's awake. How are you feeling?"

"Like I owe you my life. I'm not sure I would've made it out of that shed if it weren't for you." Blisters stung beneath the gauze, but the low dose of morphine still clinging to her sympathetic nervous system muffled the pain. The last moment of consciousness, of staring up into his face as he hauled her away from the flames, had engrained itself into her mind, and she pressed her hands into the mattress to counter the emotion that came with it. "Thank you."

"Just doing my job, Doc. Besides, I'm sure you would've done the same for me." Weston settled back into the chair, his expression solid and hurt. "I'm glad you're okay."

She nodded, unable to meet his gaze. Tears burned in her eyes, and she lowered her attention to a single thread unravelling from the heavy blanket on the bed. Her heart squeezed from the obvious pain in his eyes. She swallowed through the thickness in her throat, but there were certain pains that couldn't be healed with anything more than time. "I'm sorry about your father. He… When he saw the pickup coming toward us, he pushed me off the four-wheeler so I wouldn't be caught in the collision. James saved my life, and I'll never forget that."

"He was always one to put others' safety before his own." Silence settled between them. A minute.

Two. The heaviness he'd obviously been fighting charged to the surface. "I still remember one winter we were headed back to the ranch from picking up supplies in town. The road home was covered in at least a half inch of ice, but he'd driven that stretch so many times it was just another day for him." The police chief scrubbed a hand down his face. "An oncoming sedan slid into our lane, but instead of swerving to avoid them like most people would and going down the gulch, he slowed down, threw the truck in Reverse and aimed right for this family we could hear screaming from inside the car. My brother and I were never more scared in our lives, but James Ford simply let their car hit ours so he could help them stop. Worked, too. Everyone walked away that day."

The urge to reach out to him, to smooth the lines between his eyebrows, curled her blistered fingers into her palms. Another crack in her guard spread wider at the obvious respect he'd kept for his father, and a hit of grief crushed the air from her lungs. She knew what it was like to lose a parent—accident or not—and her heart squeezed. "Sounds like he was a great man."

"He was. My whole life I thought he was more interested in helping everyone but his own family, but now that I look back, I can see he was preparing us to do the same. To be there for the people who couldn't help themselves." Weston shifted in his seat. "Easton is working with Mom on the arrangements. They're going to try to have the funeral within the next few days."

"You should be with them. They need you." But even as she said the words—believed them with her whole heart—the hollowness in her chest throbbed with need. The need not to be alone, to have him close. The need for him to forgive her for bringing this violence and danger into his and his family's lives. These past couple days, while terrifying and filled with unimaginable loss, had shut out the loneliness she'd experienced since leaving Denver behind, and she didn't want him to go.

"I need to be here. As long as Jonathan Byrd is out there, you and the people you worked with aren't safe, and I wouldn't be any kind of police chief if I walked away from the investigation now. I've already filled in Denver PD. They're trying to get a location on the other three surgical team members who were in that surgical suite the day of Miriam Byrd's operation. There's a chance Jonathan has been so focused on you, he's temporarily given them a pass." Weston set his elbows on his knees, hands pressed together in front of him. "Chloe, look at me. Please."

The weight of his attention pressurized the air in her lungs until she gave in to her craving to look up. The combination of weariness and concern in his voice hiked her blood pressure higher, but she couldn't ignore the resulting warmth he triggered behind her rib cage.

"I need you to know I don't blame you for what happened. You are not responsible for my dad's death. Understand?" he said.

Her bottom lip shook under the swell of emotion the longer she met his gaze. "You and Easton were buried in a freezer. Your dad was killed. Everything that's happened…it's because of me. If I hadn't come to Battle Mountain—"

"He would've found you somewhere else. Maybe even killed more people to get to you." Weston rose to his feet, then maneuvered onto the edge of the bed beside her. The mattress dipped beneath his weight and pulled the left side of her body against him. Right where she needed to be. He swept callused fingers across her forehead, brushing a strand of her knotted and singed hair behind her ear, and her heart jerked in her chest. "None of this is your fault. Okay? I told you. My dad put others' safety before his own long before he met you. He knew exactly what he was doing out there. He knew a killer wanted to get to you, and he did what he had to to keep that from happening." Weston gathered her hair in one hand and swept it across her shoulders. "As for me and Easton, we got out, and being buried alive only forced us to work together to survive. You have nothing to apologize for, Doc. You're not responsible for someone else's choices, and I don't want you spending the rest of your life carrying that burden."

The hesitation she'd held on to, to keep herself from getting too close, cracked. Chloe swiped the back of her bandaged hand down her face to catch the tears escaping. "How can you just dismiss the fact none of this would've happened if I hadn't come to your town? How can you forgive me like that? You don't even know me."

"I know enough." He slid his hand down her back and planted it behind her. "We might not have known each other long and you're intense at times, maybe even a little secretive. But you're also the most intelligent, insightful and realistic woman I've ever met in my life, and I'm grateful I got the chance to work with you. I meant what I said when you were trying to sneak out of my parents' bathroom window. I can't do this without you, and I wouldn't trust anyone else to be my partner."

He leaned in close, his exhale brushing along the underside of her jaw. Anticipation coiled deep in her belly as he locked that mesmerizing gaze on her. Right before he kissed her.

HE'D NEVER KISSED another woman after his wife's death, until Chloe, and Weston couldn't keep his distance any longer. Fire scorched along his hands and up his neck as he threaded his fingers through her slightly singed hair. The flames had gotten too close.

If he'd pulled her from that shed even thirty seconds later, it would've been too late, and the tightness in his chest only intensified.

So pale against the dark blue of her borrowed scrubs, Chloe looked as though one wrong word, one tiny ding in her armor, might shatter her into a million pieces, and his entire being turned inside out.

He kissed her, falling from about a thousand feet and landing with a velvet glide of tongues that threatened to unravel every ounce of his control. Their combined exhales filled his ears, nearly drowning the pound of his pulse at the base of his skull. Electricity tornadoed into a frenzy he hadn't felt in years, but with Chloe, the low buzzing of desire had always been there and suffocated the grief clawing through him.

He'd almost lost her out there, wasn't sure what he would've done if Jonathan Byrd had finished the job he'd started three months ago, but it wouldn't have made his father proud. His family had always had his back, but this was different. She was different. She was everything he wasn't and everything he hadn't realized he'd been missing all this time. A companion, a partner, someone who'd never turn her back on him or leave.

Weston pulled back slightly, his fingers grazing her jawline. But Chloe would leave. The IV line, the blood pressure cuff, the monitor nodes and her gown—all of it had been discarded on the bed as though she hadn't planned to stick around. It made sense. Once this case was closed, she'd go back to her life in Denver. She'd slip through his fingers just as easily as Cynthia had, and he'd be alone all over again. Hell, he'd barely recovered from losing his wife. It'd taken months and hundreds of threats from his parents to pull himself out of the suffocating blackness of grief the first time. What was he doing trying to put himself back in the same position?

He wasn't ever going to leave Battle Mountain, and Chloe… She had her own life. Her own friends, a career she cared about. She'd already lost it all once. He couldn't take that from her again, but the thought of letting her go completely didn't sit well, either. He ducked his chin toward his chest and forced himself to detach as he stood. "We can't go back to the ranch. I put out an all-points bulletin to the surrounding towns up to a fifty-mile radius for Jonathan Byrd and asked residents to call in with anything suspicious, but I don't want him to be able to track you."

Overwhelming pressure took up residence under his rib cage.

"Right. No, I understand. It's… It's fine." Chloe peeled her bandaged hand from his arm and intertwined her fingers in her lap, obviously sensing the sudden distance between them. She got to her feet. "Jonathan Byrd told me he was hunting down everyone involved in his wife Miriam's death. I need to know my colleagues are safe."

"That's where you were headed when I came in the room, before I told you I had Denver PD looking for them." A rock settled in his gut, and the tight thread of anxiety that'd pushed him to find her in those woods broke.

Confusion contorted her beautiful expression. "Weston—"

His heart thundered in his chest as he collected his hat from the chair. He skimmed his fingers across the brim. "I called in a favor to get you another place. Somewhere Jonathan Bryd won't be able to connect to me or my family. You'll have everything you need until I can bring him in."

"Wait. You want to work the case alone?" she asked.

"Isn't that what you want?" He motioned to the collection of medical supplies on the bed. "Isn't that why you've been trying to run since the moment you recognized the killer's MO in the mine, and why you were getting ready to leave the hospital?"

Chloe relaxed both hands to her sides and met his gaze head-on. Her voice deadpanned, calm and guarded as it'd been the first few times they'd met. "Actually, if you'd let me finish, I could've told you I was leaving the hospital to look for you, to make sure you were okay and to figure out a way to contact my team without tipping Jonathan Byrd off."

Well, damn. He hadn't expected that. Relief replaced the pain and settled his nerves. "So then you're not planning on escaping through the bathroom window again?"

"I already checked. I won't fit through it. I'm moving on to plan B." She closed the distance between them, her full lips stretching into a heartbreaking smile he'd remember for the rest of his life. Chloe angled her hands between his arms and rib cage and secured him in a hug. Setting her head against his chest, she held on to him.

Weston pressed his mouth into the crown of her head, inhaling the residual odor of smoke and pine, and his gut clenched. "Which is?"

"I'm going to let you take me to this new safe house so I can get a proper shower, find a comfortable change of clothes since you instructed the staff to take mine as evidence, a good night's sleep and let you feed me." Her laugh reverberated through him and revitalized an easiness he hadn't let himself feel since taking the position as Battle Mountain's police chief. "I'm thinking something with pasta and cheese. Carbs and fats are the gateway of comfort food and are guaranteed to put me to sleep the fastest."

"Anything else?" He grudgingly released her and the blanket of warmth her body heat produced and offered his hand to her. "A movie perhaps or some silk pillowcases?"

Chloe slid her palm into his, and a bolt of peace filled the cracks in his wounded armor, even with the bandages over her hand. "I'll take what I can get. I might even share." Her smile disappeared as she stared up at him, and his heart kicked in his chest at the abrupt change. "Do you really think this is the best plan? Leaving your family when they need you most?"

He wasn't sure what to say to that. His family had been there for him when Cynthia had passed away. Without them, he wouldn't be where he was today, but now he was leaving them to deal with their grief alone. His mom was strong, and Easton would be there for her until Weston brought his father's killer to justice. "They understand. Come on, let's get you checked out. The longer we stay here, the higher chance Jonathan Byrd has to catch up to you."

He escorted her into the hallway, and within a few minutes she was released by the nurses at the floor's front desk. The safe house wasn't far. Maybe a twenty-minute drive, but enough distance that they might have the advantage the next time Jonathan Byrd came for her. Because he would come for her. Weston bet his entire year's salary on it. The man's hatred for the physicians responsible for his wife's death had destroyed any semblance of the husband Chloe had described. Now, there was only desperation and revenge.

They descended the stairs and exited the hospital from the east side of the building instead of the main doors. Less chance of an ambush. He threw his jacket over her shoulders and directed her toward a small black sedan on the other side of the lot. Macie had come through. He couldn't take any chances of relying on his own vehicle or anyone related to him. Not anymore.

Opening the passenger door, he helped Chloe into her seat and secured her inside. His exhales crystallized in front of his mouth with dropping temperatures as he rounded to the driver's side. Recovering the keys from the visor, he started the engine.

"Whose car is this?" Chloe took in the worn, stained upholstery, the slight hint of perfume permanently part of the vehicle and the two duffel bags in the back seat.

"Macie's." He pulled out of the hospital parking lot but didn't turn back toward the heart of town. They had to stay off the main road. It was the only way to ensure they weren't being followed. "I called her from the nurses' station, after the attending cleared me to leave, instead of using my own phone. I told her what'd happened and that we needed a vehicle that couldn't be connected back to us. Hope you don't mind, but I had her bring you a few changes of clothes, too."

She reached for the large hot-pink circular key chain knocking against his knee and smiled. A spike of desire coiled through him at the memory of those full lips under his, the softness, her taste. Honey with a hint of bite. "That explains the *coffee, choco-late and men, some things are better rich* key chain."

"Macie's very much an individualist when it comes to style. I'd take that as a warning before opening that bag she packed for you." He'd told her the truth when he said the safe house couldn't con-nect back to him. The small cabin he'd only been to once before sat at the base of Crystal Peak, northeast of town. The vehicle bounced too easily along the single dirt paved road as they wound around Lake San Cristobal. The lake had frozen over months ago, just now thawing in the middle. Colorado's second largest natural lake spanned two miles and brought in visitors from all over the state. Well-stocked with trout, it was often visited by moose hanging around the swampy shoreline and almost everyone within town during the summer. Although it'd been years since Weston had been on the water.

A single beam of sunlight pierced through the front windshield and highlighted the golden under-tones of Chloe's hair as she leaned back in her seat. No matter how many times he tried to keep his at-tention on the road, she had a certain pull he couldn't ignore. He'd felt it the moment he met her all those months ago. She was sunshine wrapped in a hurri-cane on the darkest of days, and he wasn't sure he'd ever recover—that he wanted to recover—once this investigation ended. He directed the sedan onto a smaller road heading west. Several inches of snow clung to the pines, slipping from branches as they drove up the long driveway. The trees thinned about halfway up and encircled a single structure ahead, exactly as he remembered it. He swung the car around in front of the three-story cabin and peered out the passenger side window, his chest brushing against her arm. "Let's see Jonathan Byrd find you here."

Chapter Ten

"This isn't a safe house." Chloe slammed the car door a little too firmly as she stared up at the barely standing structure punctured with two trees up through the middle. He had to be joking. "This is a treehouse."

The house featured a grand outdoor spiral staircase leading to the front door and first level, which had most likely been custom crafted around a giant Douglas fir. Above an outdoor seating area seemingly constructed with two living trees, another level stared out over the roughly five-acre lot packed with several feet of snow. A beautiful brick chimney finished the artistically designed craftsman with a shed a few yards from the base of the staircase. She'd never seen anything like it. She locked her gaze on him. "What is this place?"

With what looked like barely more than five hundred square feet of living space with two outside deck areas made from living trees, it was a cozy abode, one in which Chloe couldn't imagine staying for long without running smack into Weston multiple times. He'd kissed her at the hospital, triggering a wave of confidence and strength, a confirmation of being his equal so gut-wrenching it'd stolen her fear in an instant. Then there'd been distance, regret, as he'd backed away, and every nerve ending that'd woken in awareness of him had gone numb. She couldn't even blame him. Losing his father in the past twenty-four hours, losing his wife to cancer nearly four years ago. She couldn't imagine the battle warring inside him to rise above the grief, to move on, but she had her own skirmish tearing through her. One she hadn't expected to face when she'd come to Battle Mountain.

"I told you. Macie has a very unique outlook on life." Weston wrenched open the back door of the sedan and hauled both duffel bags from the back seat. Shouldering one, he clutched the other in his free hand. "It's not that small once you get inside. I promise."

She'd fled Denver to survive, to never have to face the helplessness being a victim had engrained in her. The only reason she'd gotten this far was by keeping her head down, moving from one town to the next and not letting herself get attached. It hurt less that way, but instead she'd found him. Weston had worked through her guard and survival instincts and reminded her how strong she could be, that she beat a killer. Twice. Now the idea of leaving Battle Mountain, of leaving him and going back to the life she'd left behind… That hurt almost as much as the stab wound in her side had. Chloe followed the divots Weston left in the snow as he trod toward the base of the outdoor staircase.

His boots thunked against the cherry-stained wood as they climbed to the first level. The entire structure had been placed on stilts, and a sudden wash of vertigo had her holding the railing tighter than necessary. Snow melted under her fingers, and she froze. The air was suddenly thinner up here, or was that her brain playing tricks on her?

"Doc? You okay?" His voice sounded too far away. Wobbly. "All the color just ran from your face."

"I don't seem to be able to move anymore." She closed her eyes against the dizziness drilling down into her bones. Her knees threatened to give out straight from under her, and in her next breath she feared she might tip over the railing. Strong hands encircled her arms, and she opened her eyes.

"Don't worry. I've got you. You've been through a lot in the past couple of days. Just hold on to me." Warm brown eyes filled her vision. He scooped her body against his and leveraged one hand against the railing. Dragging her up the last few steps, Weston refused to release her until the front door swung inward and he'd stepped over the threshold. "Almost there."

Warmth tendriled down the V-shaped collar of the scrubs she still wore and spread across her skin. The world tilted on its axis as he laid her across a red padded bench. The edges of a raw wood table swam into her vision as she set her head back. Exposed beams crisscrossed fifteen to twenty feet overhead, and as long as she focused on one of them, the dizziness ebbed. She pressed one hand against her forehead, and the blisters under the gauze screamed in warning. A modern sphere-shaped chandelier swayed, and the worst of the wooziness faded. "I'm okay. I think it's just been a while since I've eaten. My blood sugar must be low."

"It's been a while, but luckily I can take care of that. You rest. I'll get something together for us." Hands leveraged on either side of her, Weston straightened, his gaze drifting to the exposed skin above her scrub pants. His mouth parted, eyes wide, and it was then she knew. The scar. "That's a pretty nasty wound. Doesn't look very old, either."

Chloe pulled her scrub top back into place and forced herself to sit upright. The edges of her vision wobbled slightly, but not nearly as bad as it had on the stairs. The coat he'd lent her weighed heavy on her shoulders, and she slid the thick sheepskin free. Embarrassment flooded her face with heat, but the simple fact was she hadn't left Denver without a physical souvenir in addition to the mental scars she suffered whenever she closed her eyes.

"It happened the first time he attacked you, didn't it?" Weston lowered himself onto an identical bench perpendicular to hers in the small seating area. "Couldn't have been a clean stabbing. The edges are too rough for a blade."

"It was a rock." A shiver chased down her spine. The memories of that day threatened to escape the box she'd locked them inside these past few months, but she couldn't hide from them forever. "I fell while I was trying to escape. The surgeon did the best he could, but there was no way I was going to walk away without a permanent scar."

Weston hauled himself off the bench and maneuvered beside her, and her heart jumped a little higher in her chest. "Does it hurt?"

"Sometimes, but to be fair, I really haven't given it a chance to heal. As soon as the detectives informed me they weren't able to find any evidence of the attack, I checked myself out of the hospital and drove for as long and as fast as I could. It's feeling better, though. I don't wince as much when I'm cleaning the exam room at the funeral home." All those miles. All that time wasted on fearing for her life when she could've been planning a better future. Who knew she'd end up here? With him. "For what it's worth, I've felt safer here in Battle Mountain than anywhere else. Up until a few days ago, I was actually starting to accept this was where I'd end up. I have a good job, a place to live and everyone in town has been so welcoming and kind. People actually remember my name. I have a couple acquaintances outside of work and a police chief who will go to extreme lengths to protect the people under his jurisdiction. What's not to like?"

"And now?" A thread of hope infused his voice and urged her to meet his gaze.

"Now I'm not sure what's going to happen." Her throat thickened as the fear for this town that'd accepted her without hesitation twisted tighter. She'd had a plan when she'd fled Denver. Stay on the move, stay alive, but it wasn't just the town or the sense of stability that came with it that had her reconsidering the two rules that'd brought her this far. It was the thought of never finding out if this connection between her and Weston—this pull—could lead to more, to a future.

She'd had boyfriends before medical school, not really anytime during and very few after she'd graduated, but she wasn't inexperienced. There'd been late nights of passion and flirty text messages that'd rocketed her blood pressure into dangerous territory, but none of them had compared to what she'd felt when kissing him. Her lips warmed in memory. She could still taste him, the slight hint of smoked birch and peppermint, and her scalp tightened.

That moment had started a chain reaction that'd

triggered a heavy dose of desire and ended with a crushing wave of self-discovery. Her lungs emptied. Because she was in love with him. Two kisses and a hell of a lot of loyalty she didn't deserve, and she'd fallen in love with him. Chloe gripped the edge of the bench and old wood protested. "Jonathan Byrd blames me and my team for his wife's death. He won't stop until every single one of us is dead, and anyone associated with me is at risk, especially you. I can't justify you putting your life in danger for mine, but I'm grateful for everything you and your family have done for me."

Weston interlaced his hand into hers and knocked their knuckles against her outer thigh. "It's going to be okay, Doc. I've got the town on alert. Denver PD is working to put the rest of your team in protective custody, and Easton and my mom can take care of themselves. I'm not going anywhere. Understand? Your safety is my priority. Nothing else matters right now."

"Thank you." She squeezed his hand, and the tension in her rib cage released. "Now, if I remember correctly, there was talk of something to eat."

"Hope you like pancakes. They're the only food I know how to make." Bringing her hand to his mouth, he kissed the over-sensitized skin along the back of her wrist before getting to his feet. His head charged straight into the chandelier above, and he jerked out of the way with one hand secured against his skull. "I did not see that there."

Her laugh escaped easily, and for the first time in days, a weightlessness drifted through her whole body. Because of him. "That's what you get for putting me up in a tree house."

THE FIRE CRACKLED and spit embers into the clear midnight sky from the fire pit on the second deck.

No matter how many times he'd tried, Weston couldn't sleep. Not with Chloe mere inches away. He'd found a couple sleeping bags and heavy blankets tucked in the tree house's loft for the single queen-size bed, but space had become limited as soon as he'd rolled them out. He took a sip of the rich hot chocolate he'd discovered in the cupboards on the main level and let the liquid scald his mouth to counter the below-freezing temperatures. He'd let her sleep as long as possible before throwing her back into reality. The woman had survived a killer not once but twice, and there was only so much the human mind could shoulder before the cracks started to show.

His new phone pinged with an incoming message, and Weston tugged it from his coat. He and Easton had ditched their phones at the hospital. Lucky for him, his brother had serious trust issues and was able to provide him with a burner phone that couldn't be traced back to either of them or Chloe.

He read the message. No one had tried to come for Whitney Avgerpoulos's remains. The woman's family was waiting patiently for her body to be released, but it seemed Jonathan Byrd was finished with her. What Weston wouldn't give for that to be the case for Chloe.

The heavy glass door slid back on its track, and the hairs on the back of his neck stood on end. He didn't have to turn around to know how close she'd gotten. Every cell in his body had become attuned to every cell in hers in a matter of days. He sat higher in the camp chair. Hints of the perfume Macie insisted on wearing 24/7 battled with the scent of burning wood and fire. "I didn't mean to wake you up."

"You didn't. It's just colder up there without another body to warm me." Chloe maneuvered to the second chair around the fire, one of the blankets he'd found around her shoulders and a Macie-original flannel shirt and thick knitted beanie with a faux fur pom-pom completing the outfit. Tipping her head back, she stared straight up into the clear starry night as the fire cast a warm glow over her skin. "I can't remember the last time it was so…peaceful."

"Hell of a difference from Denver, I imagine." He set his mug down beside him and reached for the box of hot chocolate and dumped it into his empty cup. Careful not to burn himself, he grabbed the teakettle perched over the flames, refilled the cup and handed it to her.

"Can't say it was all bad. It's where I grew up, where my parents are buried and where I built my career. I still had friends and some family there before I left. We weren't close. Not like your family, but they were mine." She curved long fingers around the ceramic before bringing the mug up to her mouth. Closing her eyes, she inhaled the steaming liquid before taking a sip, and the danger, the investigation, the loss—it all vanished in the wash of this single moment. "Mmm. That's good."

"Secret family recipe." He held up the box and couldn't help but laugh at the ridiculousness. He tossed the rectangular cardboard box into the third camp chair and leaned back in his seat. There'd been plenty of nights just like this with his family growing up. At least once a year, usually around Christmas, they walked down to huddle around the firepit his father had built on their property. His mom would give him, Easton and his father their own hot cocoa packet, then take turns filling up each of their cups. Then she'd hand out the peppermint candy canes to stir the mix in and spice up the taste. His father would complain about burning his mouth every time, but Weston hadn't minded. It was one of the costs of his favorite night of the year. He couldn't remember the last time they'd been together like that. He'd lost Cynthia when Easton had been deployed. They'd just…let life get in the way. Now there'd be an empty seat around the fire. Weston cleared his throat as a distraction. "Easton and I were with him when he died. My dad. He'd gotten pinned between the pickup and the four-wheeler, but he hung on long enough to make sure we knew you'd been taken. Stubborn old man."

Chloe hesitated, the mug halfway to her mouth. She set it into her lap. "I wish I would've gotten to know him better. I tried going into the woods to search for you and Easton on my own, but he wouldn't let me. Told me I wasn't prepared for what I would find out there. He was right."

"He usually was. About a lot of things, whether I wanted to admit it or not. He's the one who came to me about becoming police chief after Cynthia died. I fought him at first but, as usual, I ended up taking his advice. Turned out to be one of the best decisions I've made." He could still recall the unending argument he and his dad had gotten in that day about controlling his own life, but his father had never given up on him. "Charlie Frasier was looking to retire after forty years of protecting Battle Mountain, but he didn't have anyone to replace him."

"Why not?" she asked.

"The mining companies all pulled out after they ran out of money. The economy took a turn, and people lost their jobs. Part of that mining income went to pay for the police department. When it dried up, the few deputies Frasier had on staff couldn't afford to live here anymore. Ended up taking jobs with other departments around the state." Weston stared into the flames, the warmth of the fire constant and assuring. "A few years later, Frasier had a heart attack in the middle of the station. Doctor told him his police chief days had officially come to an end. I stepped in. Seems like a lifetime ago."

"Do you regret it?" Chloe brought her legs into her chest and set her cheek against one knee, studying him from his peripheral vision. Her mug steamed from where she'd set it on the chair's arm.

"No. People rely on me to be there for them when they need it. Turns out, my father was preparing me for this my whole life. Starting with that car that slid off the road." He reached for the mug and took another gulp of hot chocolate, but he wouldn't be able to bury the loss boiling inside forever. The slightly watered-down flavor spread across his tongue. "It might be just me and Macie in that station, but the way I see it, we can still make a difference in a town this small."

"You've definitely made a difference for me." Chloe lowered her feet back to the deck and rose to stand, the blanket still wrapped around her shoulders. One step. Two. She towered over him a split second before sliding onto his lap. Warmth penetrated the icy shell that'd developed over the past hour he'd been sitting out here, and the need to keep her close took control. "If you hadn't tackled me to

the ground when that bullet ripped through the funeral home or pulled me from that burning shed, I
wouldn't be here now."

The bullet. He'd almost forgotten about the gunshot the day they'd discovered Whitney Avgerpoulos's body. Weston wrapped both arms around her
waist. "Jonathan Byrd didn't attack me with a gun
out there in those woods, and I didn't recover one
in his pickup."

"He took the one you gave me for protection."
She snaked her hands around the back of his neck
and threaded her fingers through his hair. "I meant
to tell you earlier, but—"

"I'm not worried about my gun, Chloe. His MO is
abducting and burying the people he blames for his
wife's death, not to mention the people who get in
his way, in mine and Whitney Avgerpoulos's case.
Why take a shot at you at the funeral home if he
planned to put you in that freezer?" There was something they were missing. Weston made a mental note
to message his brother to collect the bullet from the
funeral home. It'd take time, but there was a chance
ballistics could match it from the federal database
if the weapon had been used in another crime. "It
doesn't fit his pattern."

"But there was a gunshot, remember? That's why
you went into the woods in the first place. And he
didn't put me in the freezer. He buried you and

Easton and left me to burn in that shed," she said. "Jonathan Byrd isn't a serial killer. He's a man who's lost the woman he loves, and he's desperate to make that pain go away in whatever way possible. I'm not sure his mind is clear enough to follow a pattern."

She had a point. This wasn't the work of a seasoned killer. There might not be any MO to follow as far as this case was concerned, which would make Weston's job only harder. No pattern meant less predictability. "Easton came back from his last tour determined never to raise a weapon at another human being again, but he still kept one in his cabin for self-defense. According to his statement, he'd noticed movement outside his window, but knew it wasn't me or our parents."

"The family rules?" she asked.

"As long as we are on Ford land, we follow them without hesitation. For all our sakes. Easton armed himself and went to check it out. His gun discharged when Jonathan Byrd ambushed him from behind, and I found my weapon right where I'd dropped it during our altercation. No other weapons were recovered at the scene." His vision unfocused the stronger his instincts grew. Weston locked his gaze on hers. "I don't think you getting caught in that shed was his plan. At least, not entirely. There was no way he would've been able to predict Easton would get involved, but the freezer was already in place. Why take the time to bury a container that will fit two people if you only plan on killing one?"

"When I was tied up in the shed he told me the freezer was meant for me…and you," she said.

"Makes sense. He knew I was protecting you. I was the one person standing in his way to get to you. What better way to kill two birds with one stone than to bury them alive together?" The memory of slowly suffocating next to his brother charged forward. "I don't believe Jonathan Byrd shot at us two days ago."

Chloe leaned back slightly, her grip tighter than before. "Then who?"

"That's what I want to know." Weston interlaced his fingers on her opposite hip, careful of the wound she'd revealed earlier. The outline, the jaggedness to the skin, flashed across his mind every time he closed his eyes, and he wanted nothing more than to return the damage to the bastard who'd caused it in the first place. He hiked his knees higher, forcing her weight to shift against him. She settled against his chest, and he tipped his chin down to get a good long look at the coroner who'd risked her life to save his. "But not tonight. Tonight it's just us. No bullets. No freezers. No bodies. Just us and this fire."

She leveled her mouth with his, scanning his face from forehead to chin as though looking for permission to close the distance between them. "For how long?"

"As long as we need." He wanted her, and for the first time in years, he was ready. To move on, to heal. Ready for her.

Chapter Eleven

She shuddered awake.

Chloe cracked her eyes against the snow-white winter wonderland frozen all around her. Curling into the double-wide sleeping bag Weston had dragged out onto the deck once they'd finished their hot chocolate, she tried to hide from the frigid temperatures, only to realize the fire had been fed. Flames popped and crackled in uneven intervals as she clutched the edge of the sleeping bag and the heavy blanket. Goose bumps prickled down her spine as she sat up, the clothes she'd borrowed from Macie more than enough to fight back the cold.

Weston had slipped from the heap of blankets without her notice.

She skimmed her fingers across his side of the red flannel-lined sleeping bag. Still warm. He couldn't have gotten up more than a few minutes ago, but he'd given her the time to stretch and revel in a forgotten kind of muscle soreness she hadn't experienced in nearly a year. A smile pulled at one corner of her mouth as the memories of last night played in fractured sequences across her mind. The kisses against her skin, the feel of his hands memorizing every inch of her, the pleasure that'd swept her out of reality and stolen the nightmares of the past few days. He'd stripped the last of the armor she'd carried for far too long away in a matter of hours and barreled through her deepest fear: being harmed again.

No matter how many times she'd tried to convince herself otherwise, Weston got to her. Committed. Reliable. Willing to defend her until the end. He was nothing she'd expected when she'd come to Battle Mountain and everything she wanted in her life, and despite the timing and their situation, she'd already started falling in love with him.

The large glass door separating the tree house from the great outdoors slid back on its track, and every sense she owned homed in on him.

"Good morning. Hope you're hungry." His boots reverberated through the wood underneath her. Rich brown hair tussled to one side as he maneuvered through the door with two plates in his hands.

Chloe straightened. She took in his thick coat and strong thighs beneath his sweatpants. "Starving."

He stretched one plate of steaming food toward her. "We can go inside if you prefer."

She accepted the plate and breathed in the combination of pancakes, butter, maple syrup and sausage links. "I'm still pretty warm after last night, thanks to you." Chloe balanced the plate on top of the sleeping bag and dove straight in. She couldn't remember the last time someone other than his mother had made her a home-cooked meal. Most of her meals had been in the clinic cafeteria, considering she'd worked twelve-to-eighteen-hour days, and the food she'd kept at home stayed fresh in the freezer. The sweetness of the maple syrup coated her tongue. Who knew being hunted by a man who'd lost his hold on reality could come with so many benefits? "This is really good."

Weston took his seat in the camp chair they'd shared the night before. "I feel like I should warn you. Macie only eats breakfast food, so her pantry and fridge are stocked with pretty much everything you'd possibly want in the morning. And that's it."

"She lives here full-time?" Chloe recalled the single time she'd met the friendly redheaded dispatcher at Caffeine and Carbs, and now that she thought about it, she could definitely picture the woman living life on her own terms. "It's very generous of her to let us stay here and rummage through her kitchen. You might want to tell her she's going to need to wash these sleeping bags, though."

His laugh encircled her in a hug of warmth and lightness and stirred hints of the heat he'd stoked low in her belly. He took a bite of his own food, a string of syrup catching in his beard. "I think I'll wash them myself and leave her out of it. If she even gets a hint I've been with someone, I'll never hear the end of it. The woman has been trying to set me up for years."

"I didn't realize you hadn't been with anyone after your wife passed." The small amount of hope this could be something more exploded through her. Chloe set her fork on the plate, the ding of stainless steel against ceramic too loud in her ears.

His smile left his expression. "When Cynthia died, I cut myself off from my friends, my family, her family. I got stuck in this cycle of grief I couldn't seem to pull myself out of until I took this job, but even then I wasn't ready to let myself get attached to anyone. Until I met you."

"You think I'm worth getting attached to?" She hadn't meant for the question to slip past her control, but there it was. Her heart, her future, on the line and exposed for the world to see.

"Is that a problem?" he asked.

"No." She shook her head. Butterflies stirred in her stomach. "Not at all. I'm kind of attached to you, too."

Weston used the side of his fork to cut another section of pancake but didn't take a bite. Veins threatened to escape the callused skin along the backs of his hands as he stared down at the contents on his plate. "So what do you think you'll do after we've caught Jonathan Byrd and this investigation is over?"

"I don't know." She stretched her feet toward the bottom of the sleeping bag, aware he held all the cards here. Physically, mentally, emotionally. "I ran from my life in Denver to survive. I trusted the detectives there to find the man who tried to kill me, even after all these months, but I knew they'd given up due to lack of evidence. I certainly didn't think I'd be here trying to catch him. I guess I've never really thought about what would happen or where I would go afterward."

He didn't move, didn't even seem to breathe, and the tension between them tightened. He was waiting for an answer, waiting for her to choose him. She could see it in his eyes, in the set of his mouth.

Chloe set down her plate on the slightly frosted deck, her fork skimming across the ceramic. "Battle Mountain has been my home for the past two months. There's something about this town that made me want to get to know the people here and stop running. I have a good job and an apartment I can turn into my own. Where else can I actually get a barista to write my name correctly on my cup?"

That earned her a smile, and her heart shot into her throat. "You make a good point."

She hugged her knees into her chest to counter the bite of early spring mornings and the instant reaction he seemed to pull from her with one look.

"Honestly, I think I would like it here as long as I had someone to enjoy it with." His expression softened under her admission, and her pulse beat faster. "To be clear, I mean you."

"I was hoping you'd say that." Weston shoved to his feet. He tossed his plate into his vacated chair, and she looked up just in time as he closed in on her. He threaded his arms underneath her knees and low back, gathering the sleeping bag and blanket, and swept her off the deck. Tendons in his neck flexed under her weight, but he barely missed a step as he maneuvered her through the sliding glass door.

A wall of warmth encased her as he used his heel to slide the door closed behind them. She wrapped her arms around his neck but still struggled to keep her balance as he hauled her up to the second level without any sign of exertion. "What are you—"

The tree house blurred in her vision as he tossed her onto the single queen-size bed, and a squeak of surprise escaped past her lips. She clutched the sleeping bag tighter around her.

The mattress dipped under the weight of his knee as he crawled to meet her in the middle, his weight seemingly the only thing keeping her anchored in the moment. Threading one hand through the hair at the back of her neck, Weston brought her mouth to meet his, and the world, the investigation, the grief for an entire life she'd lost disappeared. There was only him. "I didn't think I'd ever find someone

I trust as much as I trust myself. Then I met you. You're the most persistent, straight-talking, challenging woman I've ever met, Doc. You're everything I've been missing all these years. I've taken an oath to protect this town and everyone in it, but I'm not sure I'd survive if something ever happened to you."

"Good thing you don't have to worry about that. Because I'm not going anywhere." She pressed her mouth to his, framing both hands along his jaw, and brought him up to settle his weight onto her. Her chest ached at the thought of how much he'd already lost, but she could be here for him now. As long as Jonathan Byrd couldn't hurt them that would never change. "But I need you to promise me something first, Weston."

A furrow developed between his brows, and he leveraged his weight into his hands on either side of her shoulders. "What is it?"

"I'm not her." Chloe smoothed her thumb over the thick sheepskin lining of his coat at his collar. "I'm not your wife, and I don't ever want you to believe I could fill that space you still have for her in your heart. She was such a big part of your life, and I don't want you to stop loving her. She deserves better than that, and so do I. Promise me, that whatever this is between us, it doesn't have anything to do with her. Promise me you'll keep her memory alive but see me as…me."

A corner of his mouth quirked into a smile. "Hell, woman, I think I just fell a little bit in love with you."

"Promise me." The words left her mouth as nothing more than a whisper but held the weight of their entire future. She curled her bandaged hand into his coat. "Please."

Weston kissed her, sweeping his tongue past the seam of her lips, before setting his forehead against hers. "I promise."

THE GRATING PING of a cell phone shoved him back into consciousness.

Water ticked against tile from the only bathroom with a shower. A wall of humidity bellowed into the bedroom from the cracked door a few feet from the bed, and Weston scrubbed a hand down his face. He reached for the small clock radio on the raw wood nightstand built into the wall and knocked into the lamp instead. Shooting one hand out, he caught the damn thing before it hit the floor. "I'm awake."

The burner phone pinged again.

Ten in the morning. Damn, he'd passed out after showing Chloe exactly how much she'd meant to him over these past few days. He'd never slept so well in his life despite the grief simmering below the surface, and the pull of drugging sleep urged him to collapse back into bed, to forget anything that existed outside this ridiculous safe house. The sleeping bag and blanket they'd taken refuge under last night on the deck had slid to the floor, and he hauled himself upright before tossing both back onto the bed. He stood, knees popping at the effort, and shuffled down the winding staircase to the main level. The phone vibrated on the butcher-block countertop in the wraparound kitchen, and he slammed a hand down over it. Easton had moved on to calling him. Hitting the green button to connect, he brought the phone to his ear. "Yeah, what is it?"

"You've got another body on your hands." His brother's voice deadpanned. "You need to get back into town. Now."

"What do you mean another body?" The words replayed over in his head, but it took longer than it should have to make sense. Weston turned and raised his gaze to the second level, the constant white noise of the shower steady. "Jonathan Byrd is hunting Chloe and the rest of her surgical team. I can't leave her alone here, and I'm sure as hell not bringing her back into town to make her an easier target than she already is."

"That won't be a problem," Easton said. "Not anymore."

"What are you talking about?" he asked.

"I just found Jonathan Byrd's remains. I'm not a detective but he was murdered, from the look of it." Soft footsteps echoed through the line, then the sound of a passing car. Easton was on the move, most likely down Main Street. "I went back to Jacob

Family Funeral Home to recover the bullet like you'd asked. Don't worry. I was careful. I pulled the discarded slug from the wall and bagged it without getting my prints on the evidence, but as I was leaving, I noticed the dead bolt to the exam room Chloe works out of had fresh scratches on the lock face. Someone had picked the lock. Horribly, I might add. The victim you found, Whitney Avgerpoulos, you told me you'd asked Frank Jacob to secure the remains after the shooting, so I thought maybe your suspect had come looking for her. Turns out, your suspect was there instead."

"Jonathan Byrd is dead." Weston gripped the edge of the counter. Son of a bitch. "How?"

"There's a bullet wound between his eyes. Entry wound looks to be the same caliber as the bullet I'm holding right now. Can't be sure until your coroner examines the body, but he was definitely tortured first," Easton said. "Whoever killed him wanted something."

"Chloe." Movement registered from above. His grip slipped from around his phone as Chloe stared down at him from the second floor. He caught the device just before it fell past his waist and brought it back to his ear. Not really paying attention to anything his brother said on the other end of the line. "I need to call you back."

He ended the call.

Wrapped in a clean white robe, hair dripping

around her shoulders, she descended the stairs, every inch the woman who'd penetrated his strongest defenses and broken him down to nothing. She hit the bottom of the stairs, one hand still gripping the railing as though preparing for the worst. "Something's happened."

"That was Easton. I sent him back to the funeral home to recover the bullet from the shooting so we could run ballistics." They'd known exactly who'd targeted her all those months ago, what kind of monster had driven her to flee Denver and go on the run for her life. Only now a new monster had stepped from the shadows, one they didn't know anything about.

"Okay." She folded her arms across her chest. "Did he find it?"

"Yes, but he found something else while he was there." He set the phone back on the counter and braced himself. "Jonathan Byrd's body. Someone tortured and killed him, presumably to get information from him."

"Information? What...kind of information?" The small muscles along her throat constricted with a hard swallow.

"As of right now, I think we need to assume it has to do with you." His stomach knotted tighter. They'd had him. The Creed and Silverton police departments had cut off Jonathan Byrd's escape by setting up roadblocks along both roads leading in and out of Battle Mountain, but now the game had changed. There was a new player, and they'd been forced back to square one. "Jonathan Byrd wasn't able to kill you. There's a chance he had a partner we didn't know about who's out to finish the job."

The color drained from her face, that full bottom lip he'd memorized with a dozen kisses merely an hour ago pulling away from the top. She shifted her weight back, and Weston closed the distance between them in case she collapsed. "This doesn't make sense. He was the one who attacked me in Denver. He was the one who buried you and Easton and killed your father. He left me in that shed to die. Now you're saying he was murdered by someone else."

He wound his arms around her waist and held her tighter than ever before. "Until we're able to determine when and how he officially died, you need to stay here—"

"No." She shook her head, all that dark brown hair sticking to her robe. "I can't do this. I can't spend the rest of my life looking over my shoulder. That's not a life, Weston. That's fear, and I've been letting it control me for too long." Chloe dug her fingernails into his arms. "I can't hide from this anymore. You asked me to stay and help you solve this case. That's what I'm doing."

He nodded, knowing exactly what she'd say next.

"I need to examine the body." Chloe maneuvered

out of his arms as acceptance smoothed her expression. Tugging the robe tighter around her frame, she pushed wet hair out of her face. "I know that means leaving the safe house. I know that means putting my life at risk, but I trust you'll do whatever it takes to make sure I walk away from this alive."

Weston pulled her into his arms, and she melted into him. Running one hand down the thick waterfall of her hair, he clung to her as the last moments of Cynthia's life filled his head. The hollowness that'd carved into his chest that day ebbed, and for the first time in years, he was able to take a full breath. "I can't lose you."

"You won't." Pulling back, she squeezed his arms in reassurance. "But as much as I enjoyed last night under the stars, I'm not walking outside naked. I'm going to get dressed in every layer Macie owns."

His laugh escaped up his throat easily, and Weston forced his hands to release her. He waited until she'd ascended the stairs and the sound of the bathroom door closing behind her reached his ears. Collecting the burner phone from the counter, he called his brother. The line rang once. Twice. He didn't wait for a greeting as the call connected. "Where are you?"

"Across the street from the funeral home. I'm watching to see if anyone comes back to visit their handiwork." Easton spoke over the rush of cars along Main. "The guy could've easily bypassed the front door since the glass hasn't been replaced from your shooting yet. He had everything he needed to extract the information he wanted in that exam room. Looks like the bastard put it all to use, too. I reached out to a couple of contacts in Denver. He was a handyman. No military or law enforcement training. It wouldn't have taken long to get him to give up whatever they wanted from him, but I'm not going to lie. It's a mess in there."

"You're saying it's possible whoever killed Jonathan Byrd kept torturing him, even after he gave them the information they wanted." Hell. There was only one reason to inflict that much pain on another human being: rage. The pressure of three murders crushed the air from his lungs, almost as though he and Easton had been buried all over again. He'd put his family in danger long enough, but he didn't have the manpower or the resources to solve this case alone. Weston leveraged one hand against the live tree shooting up through the roof in the center of the living space. Rough bark scratched at his palms. "Listen, I was wrong before, Easton. These past few months I thought you'd given up, that you wished you'd been in that explosion rather than the men and women in your unit. I hated seeing you waste away in that cabin day after day when Mom, Dad and I were right there willing to do anything to help. We were best friends before you shipped out on orders, and I didn't understand why you couldn't just try to move on and be my brother again. I understand now. You're punishing yourself."

Weston tightened his grip on the phone. "I can't tell you you're not the one responsible for what happened to your unit. I can't promise you you'll heal. I wish I had the answers and that I could help you. I wish I could take away that guilt, but that's something you need to confront yourself. Just as I had to when Cynthia died. I know what I'm supposed to do now, and I need your help. I've already asked a lot of you, and we've had our differences over the years, but I can't do this without you, brother. I need you on my side now. I need you to help me protect this town and the people in it."

Silence bled through the line. His heart threatened to beat out of his chest, and Weston set his forehead against the tree, waiting. Memories of him and Easton growing up had been overrun by the anger, hurt and disappointment of the past six months, but right then none of it mattered. They were brothers. They'd get through this. Just as their father had taught them.

Easton's voice penetrated through the slight ringing in his ears. "Tell me what you need me to do, Chief."

Chapter Twelve

The Jacob Family Funeral Home looked almost exactly the same, yet everything had changed. In a matter of days, her new life had been ripped out of her control and turned into something she didn't recognize.

Chloe stepped through the empty glass door frame. Weston's brother had sent the bullet to the forensic lab in Denver, but it would be days, if not weeks, before any kind of ballistic results came back, and only if the gun had been used in a previous crime. Whomever Weston had asked to repair the door had swept away the glass, but the weight of standing here, of knowing exactly who was on the other side of the examination room door, cut through her as sharply as though she hadn't worn boots.

Bright scratches stood stark against the brushed nickel of the dead bolt lock face securing her room. Jonathan Byrd's killer had brought his victim here, tortured him for some kind of information and killed him when he was finished. Her hand hesitated over the doorknob, her heart in her throat. He'd wanted to send her a message.

"You okay?" Weston's voice soothed the rough edges of her nerves. "I can call another coroner in from Silverton or Ouray."

"No." She shook her head. She could do this. She had to do this. She pushed inside. A wall of odor slammed into her. Upon death, the cells in the human body broke down and released gasses, coppery and fruity at the same time, and her stomach lurched. Dried red and crusted brown spatter arced across the walls, counter and cabinets, but the source of the blood was what consumed her attention. Jonathan Byrd had been strapped against her stainless-steel exam table with what looked like two stained yellow furniture straps, one across his chest, the other across the thighs. His hands had also been secured, a third strap encircling each wrist before diving beneath the table and tightened to full capacity.

Awareness of Weston warmed the skin down her back as he moved inside the small room with her. It'd been only a few days ago he'd stood right here and handed her coffee. Their fingers had brushed against one another, and she'd gotten that burst of attraction she'd cut herself off from so long ago. Now here they were, standing over the remains of another victim, him on one side of the room, her beside the table. What she wouldn't give to go back to that moment of blatant denial that Whitney Avgerpoulos's death had just been a coincidence. She knew the truth now.

Chloe mentally inventoried the surgical instruments Jonathan Byrd's killer had used during the torture and the kit they'd come from at the end of the counter. Her medicolegal kit. Every single one of these tools were hers, and the realization pooled dread at the base of her spine. Willingly or not, she'd played a part in this man's death. Pulling a fresh set of latex gloves into place, she watched where she stepped and unpocketed her phone. Just as she'd done at the scene where Whitney had been buried, she took photos.

"Does anything stand out to you? Anything that might tell us who we're dealing with?" Weston's voice dipped an octave.

"There's an outline of a phone in the victim's pocket. The killer primarily used the scalpel over there on that cart, judging by the width of these wounds and the amount of blood on the instrument. These are my tools. They're all from that kit. I left it here after Whitney Avgerpoulos's autopsy. I usually keep it in the trunk of my car." She surveyed the lacerations across the killer's—the victim's—thoracic, abdominal and pelvic cavities. Dozens, all of varying depths and lengths, which suggested more of a swiping motion rather than a premeditated incision. Whoever'd done this had wanted Jonathan Byrd to suffer as much as possible. "Considering the bullet between his eyes, I'm leaning toward gunshot wound to the head. Manner of death is homicide."

"When?" Weston asked.

A burning exhale escaped as she raised her gaze to the victim's face. Agony had contorted his features in his last moments, and her heart shuddered in her chest. Jonathan Bryd had killed her colleague, attacked Chloe in Denver, had tried to bury her and ripped the life she'd worked so hard for away in a single instant. He'd buried Weston and his brother alive, killed a man willing to sacrifice himself to ensure she made it out alive and stole the life of an innocent young woman—all to ease the rage over his wife's death. She'd feared for her life while comprehending the source of his hatred. In a way, she'd understood him. But this… This wasn't pain. This wasn't grief or revenge. This was animalistic, and nothing she'd ever seen before.

Weston's hand spread across her shoulder blade. "Chloe?"

"I won't be able to give you an exact time frame without an autopsy, but right now I'm confident he was killed approximately eight to twelve hours ago." While she and Weston were whispering promises of the future and losing themselves to ecstasy. Chloe took the last of the photos and handed her phone off to Weston. Some items in her kit hadn't been disturbed, but to use or move anything inside it now might compromise the investigation. A rough stab wound claimed her attention, and she spread the skin on either side wider to get a better view. "This wound is more jagged than all the others. Rougher. Most likely the strike that incapacitated him. The scalpel was driven deep enough to hit the kidney, but that kind of force would most likely dislodge the killer's grip. His hand would've slid down the blade, maybe even cut himself in the process. I'll need cotton swabs and evidence bags to collect samples, some tweezers, and booties so I don't contaminate the scene."

"I'll check with Mr. Jacob and see what I can recover from the phone's call history." Weston unpocketed the phone from the victim's front pocket and flipped the old device open. He left the room and headed down the corridor, presumably toward Mr. Jacob's office, and all four walls seemed to close in around her.

Four bodies. So much pain. Her fingers curled into the center of her bandaged palms, and she stared down at the blisters peeking out from the stretched edges of gauze and under the latex gloves. Jonathan Byrd had wanted her and her colleagues to suffer for the death of his wife, but she couldn't do that to the people of this town, to Weston. She couldn't keep risking their lives for her mistake. Chloe slid one foot toward the door. The streaks of blood arcing over the walls and cabinets seemed to pulse right in front of her. Whoever'd done this had known exactly where to strike the victim. They were familiar with human anatomy and comfortable with a scalpel and used that knowledge to torture and kill her attacker for information. Who would they target next to tie up loose ends? Mr. Jacob? Easton or Karie? Her throat swelled with a pent-up sob. Weston?

No. Her heart threatened to beat straight out of her chest as she took another step. Every nerve ending in her body caught fire as images of Weston replaced the face of the victim on the table. The blood pooling beneath the body didn't belong to the man who'd attacked her out in those woods, who'd killed James Ford and Whitney Avgerpoulos and Roberta Ellis. All she could see was Weston. Nausea churned in her gut as her spine met the door frame, and she jerked to a stop. He'd promised to protect her, to solve this case together, but the rules to the sick game Jonathan Byrd started had changed. There was a new piece of the puzzle to solve, and she feared neither of them would survive to see the finished picture. She couldn't stay here. Not as long as her proximity to Weston, to his family, this town was the one element putting them in danger.

She had to move. Chloe peeled her gloves from her hands with a snap and discarded them in the trash can by the door. She escaped the exam room and forced one foot in front of the other, picking up her pace with every step. The hairs on the back of her neck prickled as cool air guided her toward the front door. Tears burned in her eyes, but she wouldn't let them fall. Not yet. Weston had left the keys trapped in the driver's side visor of Macie's sedan. She could make it.

"I think I've got everything you need, Doc." His voice stabbed straight through her, but Chloe refused to slow down. A hint of panic infused his tone, and something struck the floor at the end of the hallway. "Chloe?"

She raced through the broken front door without bothering with the metal handle and pumped her legs as hard as she could. Her lungs seized as heavy footsteps pounded loud behind her. She didn't stop to see how close he'd gotten. Ripping open the driver's side door of the sedan, she collapsed into the vehicle, collected the keys from the visor and inserted the key into the ignition. Movement registered from the sidewalk a split second before she thought to lock the doors.

Weston slammed both hands onto the hood of the vehicle, those mesmerizing brown eyes locked on her, and her entire body flinched. "Don't do this, Chloe."

"I'm sorry. For everything." She shifted the car into Reverse and slammed on the accelerator. The vehicle lurched out from beneath the police chief's weight, and she swung into the middle of Main Street. Residents stared as she slammed the car into

Drive. The tires screamed in protest but caught the pavement and shot her forward.

Weston's outline ran straight for her door out of her peripheral vision. He tried the handle but wasn't able to keep up as she sped from the scene. Within seconds, he centered himself in the rearview mirror, both hands interlaced behind his head, and her heart shattered.

The tears flowed down her cheeks the more distance she put between them, but she wouldn't stop. Couldn't. Thick green trees dissolved to open fields and rolling hills. She wasn't sure where she was going, how far she'd get on half a tank of gas or how she'd pay for her next meal. It didn't matter. She'd started over once before. She could do it again.

A single vehicle stretched across the road ahead, red and blue lights working to overcome the sun's morning rays, and her chest squeezed. The roadblocks. Weston had called in other departments from nearby towns to box Jonathan Bryd in. Chloe swallowed around the panic clawing up her throat. Had Weston radioed them to stop her?

She forced Macie's old sedan to slow to a crawl as she approached the single officer climbing from his patrol vehicle. Within a few seconds, he tapped his baton against the driver's side window and signaled for her to roll it down. She did, every cell in her body praying he'd let her through.

"Good morning, ma'am. We're looking for a

wanted suspect in a homicide investigation. Mind if I see your license and search your vehicle?" the officer asked, wrinkles putting his age somewhere close to sixty if she had to guess.

Chloe unpocketed her fake license with her assumed name from her jacket pocket and handed it to him, hands trembling. "I don't mind. The car's not mine. I'm borrowing it from a friend. Macie Barclay? You might know her. She's the dispatcher here in Battle Mountain."

"Sure, I know Macie." He read the details of her license and holstered his baton. "Everything all right, ma'am? You look as though you've been crying."

A car horn from behind jolted her nervous system into overdrive, and she clenched the steering wheel harder. The officer waved as she checked the rearview mirror, half expecting Weston's truck. Instead, a darker truck, dark blue or black, revved its engine. Without much traffic out of town, they were the only two vehicles on the road.

"I'm fine. Thank you." She swiped at her face. "Long day is all. I'd really like to get going if you don't mind."

A second man materialized behind the officer, pulled the firearm from his belt and slammed the butt of the gun against the officer's head. The old man crumpled, and in her next breath, the attacker aimed the gun at her. "Hello, Dr. Miles. I'm so glad I was finally able to catch up with you."

DAMN IT ALL to hell. Chloe was gone.

The watery outline of Macie's sedan dipped below the horizon. He could radio the officer set up at the roadblock. He could stop her. But what would be the point? She'd made her decision, and she was an expert at running. Weston threw his hat against the pavement. What the hell had he expected? A car drove past, reminding him he was still standing in the middle of Main Street with another body on his hands. She'd left him. Despite her promise she wasn't going anywhere, she'd left him. And he wanted to know why. "Son of a bitch."

He'd already lost his wife, lost his father. Now Chloe. The hollowness in his gut exploded, destroying the security and support that'd built up over the past few days with her at his side. She'd made it clear from the beginning. She'd wanted to run the moment they'd pulled Whitney Avgerpoulos from that mine, and the burn of abandonment and betrayal shot his blood pressure into dangerous territory. Worse, she was out there, on the run, alone, while another killer had obviously gone out of his way to tie up loose ends.

Weston bent down to collect his hat and headed back inside Jacob Family Funeral Home to contain the scene. The only person able to tell them who'd strapped Jonathan Byrd to an exam table and tortured him until he'd bled to death had fled. He'd have to call in another coroner or a nearby medical examiner to complete the autopsy. He needed that evidence to find the bastard who'd killed their killer. The odor of death and decomposition drove into his lungs. Holding his breath, he pulled the phone from his jacket and froze. Chloe's phone, the one she'd used to take photos of the scene. She'd handed it off to him before sending him to get supplies to collect the evidence. She'd known, even then, he would've used it to track her whereabouts. So she'd gotten rid of it.

He dug for the burner phone in his coat and hit the only contact number stored in the memory. The line connected. No small talk. They were running out of time. "Tell me you were able to find something I can use."

"Both Gregory and Delphine Avgerpoulos were at the restaurant until late last night. I have statements from one of the busboys and the dishwasher corroborating they didn't leave until 2:00 a.m. this morning," Easton said. "Neither of them are your killer, and Mom slapped me when I asked her if she'd tortured anyone lately. None of them even knew what'd happened until I told them."

Relief fought to cool the rage that'd taken control. Of all the people who'd had a motive to want Jonathan Byrd dead, he'd had to consider Whitney's parents and his own mother. "Good. You got that bullet sent to Unified Forensics?"

"Just left the post office. I'm headed your way. Almost there," Easton said.

Weston scanned the hallway, targeting the medical supplies he'd dropped chasing after Chloe. "Meet me in the exam room. We've got work to do."

He hung up and picked up the swabs, bags, tweezers and booties. The phone he'd taken from the victim's pocket had logged only one call. To the Battle Mountain police station. Jonathan Byrd had placed the anonymous call informing dispatch of Whitney Avgerpoulos's body in Contention Mine. He'd still pull prints and run them against the database, but now he had proof the man on that table had a hand in a young woman's death. Unpacking the booties, he slipped one over each boot. Footsteps echoed down the hallway before Easton appeared at his side. He handed off another set of booties and waited for his brother to finish before handing him a set of swabs and bags.

Easton stared down at the supplies, then seemed to comprehend exactly what Weston intended for them to do. "When I said I'd help you with this case, I didn't mean getting my hands bloody. Where's your coroner?"

"She's not mine." The words left his mouth harsher than he'd intended. No matter what his current feelings for the woman who'd worked her way into his life, he had a job to do, and he couldn't wait for another town to send someone. "I watched Dr. Miles swab for evidence from Whitney Avgerpoulos's body in the mine. We've already got pictures. Now we need to collect anything that might tell us who did this."

Dr. Miles. Her formal title bit like acid on his tongue.

"Her name's not Chloe Pascale." Easton's easy acceptance of that truth punctured as loud as the snap of latex gloves over his hands. "Didn't seem the type to lie about that kind of thing, but given the fact she obviously came here to hide from the pincushion on the table, can't say I blame her."

"There were a lot of things she convinced us were true." Weston swabbed around the wound in Jonathan Byrd's knee and bagged the evidence. He handed it off to his brother and continued examining the remains. Silence descended between them as they worked. He didn't want to get into what'd happened between him and Chloe, and Easton wasn't the type to pry. Made things easier for now. He mapped out the pattern of wounds, but the wound she'd pointed out before, rougher than the others, stood out among the rest. "All of these across the abdomen are superficial. Like they were for show." He pointed to the smallest of the collection. "Chloe was focused on this particular wound before she left. She said the killer had used so much force, it was possible he'd cut his hand. I'm no coroner, but as far as I know, nobody can survive a direct strike to the kidney like that for long, can they?"

"You're right. It's slightly wider than the others." Easton leaned over the body. "Most likely made with the same weapon, but the killer twisted the scalpel after piercing the kidney. Your victim here never would've recovered. Whoever got to this guy knew exactly how to make sure he'd never escape until he was finished."

Special Forces? Weston scanned the remains for something—anything—that would fill the empty segments of this case forming in his mind. What were the chances Battle Mountain had become a hunting ground for not one but two killers within the span of a week? A theory patched together as he recalled the reason Chloe had been targeted in the first place. She was going to report the surgical team's mistake to the board of the clinic. She was going to take responsibility for Miriam Byrd's death. "Or maybe someone familiar with human anatomy?"

"I can see the wheels spinning in your head," Easton said.

"How did Jonathan Byrd know where to find Chloe after all these months? He's a handyman with a preference for '50s-era refrigerators. Doesn't seem like the kind of job where you'd have a lot of connections or the kind of resources he'd need to figure out she'd changed her name. That kind of work wouldn't have given him access to the propofol he used to sedate his victims unless he took contracts with hospitals, which I couldn't see in any of his previous work orders." Weston swabbed the area around the final wound and bagged the evidence. "He had help."

Easton straightened. "Someone gave him the coroner's location here in Battle Mountain, then set him loose, knowing he was going to kill her. Only when Whitney Avgerpoulos finds him trying to break into your doc's apartment, he has to take care of her. He blows the element of surprise, and now his target knows he's in town."

"Jonathan Byrd filed a malpractice suit the day before Chloe was attacked. She hadn't told the board what she and her team had done yet. So how did he find out, and why would he file the suit if he planned on killing her? So he can claim his innocence just in case he's accused of murder? I think someone got to him." It was the only scenario that made sense. "Chloe swore Jonathan Byrd wasn't the kind of man prone to violence, but as you and I both know, grief can change a person. Especially if that anger and resentment is fed rather than faced. Manipulating someone else's grief to act is a good way to keep your own hands clean if you don't want to be connected to a murder."

"Only problem is Jonathan Byrd failed. Chloe escaped. Twice," Easton said.

"And the puppet master has come to finish the job. I think I know who tortured and killed Jonathan Byrd, but it's going to take some time to prove it." Time he didn't have. His phone's ring pierced through the haze clouding anything outside this room. Weston ripped one glove from his hand and unpocketed the burner. "It's Macie." He swiped his thumb across the screen. "Yeah."

"Get out to the east roadblock. Now," Macie said.

Ice worked down his spine. He glanced up at Easton. "What happened?"

"Silverton PD just reported an officer down. It looks as though he'd stopped someone and was in the process of checking their identification when he was hit from behind." Macie's voice quaked. "Whoever it was took the officer's weapon."

Damn it. Battle Mountain and nearly every resident in its borders believed in the second amendment and made no qualms about showing it. Who the hell would attack a single officer just for his weapon? "Macie, I'm in the middle of collecting evidence off a fresh body. Silverton PD is going to have to take point—"

"There's more," Macie said. "He was still holding a driver's identification when Silverton PD found him, and they pulled the registration in the glove compartment of the vehicle she was driving."

She? Tension pulled the muscles tight across his back. "Spit it out."

"It's Chloe, Chief." Regret simmered beneath the dispatcher's words. "The car they found abandoned at the checkpoint is mine, but Chloe's gone."

Weston ended the call and stripped the latex gloves from his hands, depositing them in the garbage can near the door. "Secure this room. No one comes in or out aside from you."

"Something's happened." Easton's voice remained even despite the obvious change in Weston's tone. "I can help."

"Keep collecting the evidence. There has to be something here that will tie us to the killer." Weston unholstered his sidearm from his hip, released the magazine, counted the bullets and slammed it into place. He pulled back on the slide and loaded a round into the chamber, then reholstered his weapon. As much as he trusted Easton to have his back after what they'd been through together, this was something he had to do on his own. Only Chloe had taken the vehicle they'd come into town in together, and his truck was still parked up at the ranch. "Keys."

No questions. No hesitation. Easton pulled his keys from his jeans and tossed them right at him. He caught them, and in his next breath, headed for the front door. Cold dissipated as determination—stronger than anything he'd felt before—burned beneath his skin. "I'm coming for you, Doc."

Chapter Thirteen

"You should've kept up your end of the deal, Chloe," a familiar voice said. "After all, you're not the only one who has everything to lose."

Muted sunlight warmed her face through the clouds above as she pulled her head away from one shoulder. An ache snaked through the tendons in her neck. She'd been unconscious. The last few moments of memory washed across her mind in waves. The roadblock. The officer who'd been checking her ID. The shadow behind him. Her heart rate ticked up a notch. He'd pulled her from the car, then pressed something into her rib cage and everything…had gone black. A taser?

Chloe set her head back against something solid, and the thud vibrated loud in her ears. Her shoulder sockets ached under pressure. She pulled at her wrists to bring them around to the front, but plastic dug into her skin. Zip ties. She rolled her head against whatever was behind her, back and forth, but it didn't lighten the shadows across the man's face any more. A slight breeze pushed her hair into her eyes. "Where… Where am I?"

"Somewhere that police chief of yours will never find you." Her abductor stood from his crouched position a few feet in front of her, and the shadows cleared. Recognition flared as he settled dark eyes on her, and she pressed her heels into the ground to put as much distance between them as possible.

"You?" The blood drained from her face. "You did this?"

"I had some help, as you know. What better way to make sure you couldn't go to the board than to convince the patient's husband he needed to take matters into his own hands?" Michael Kerr, the resident surgeon who'd assisted her during Miriam Byrd's surgery, blocked the sun from her eyes. Stubble shaded a square jaw, which struggled to hide a layer of fat. Long, thick eyebrows, matching the light brown hair receding up his forehead, spiked in different directions, and accented a deranged set to his mouth. Crooked smile lines ended at the base of a wide nose broken at least once over the course of a forty-five-year life. He fanned his grip over the handgun at his side. Not the officer's weapon he used to knock the man unconscious. A .38 revolver she bet would match ballistics to the bullet shot at her and Weston when they'd been standing inside the Jacob Family Funeral Home and the entry wound set between Jonathan Byrd's eyes. Blood dried underneath his nose from where she'd struck him back at the roadblock. "We had a deal, Chloe. You broke that deal."

She shook her head. "I never went to the board about what happened."

"But you were going to, right?" He settled in front of her, his knees popping under his weight. Crusted dirt kicked up around him, a bright smudge of dust against his shined shoes. "You told Roberta Ellis you didn't feel right about keeping the patient's husband in the dark about what'd happened, that you couldn't lie to him. That you felt guilty for that woman's death. So what did you do? You went against the family's wishes, and you performed your own autopsy to find out what went wrong."

"Of course, I felt guilty," she said. "She died because of us. Because we left a clamp inside her chest. She was trying to tell us, but she could barely even speak she was in so much pain. We deserve to answer for what we've done." Her instincts kicked her in the gut, and she pulled her knees into her chest. The zip ties bit into her skin and wouldn't give way. Jonathan Byrd learning her location, his access to propofol… It all made sense. "It was you. The clamp. It was yours, wasn't it? You didn't want the truth coming out. You told Jonathan Byrd what really happened to his wife. He filed the lawsuit against me, but you played on his grief. You turned him into a killer, even with the possibility he'd come after you. Why?"

A thin smile contorted the laugh lines carved into his features but didn't reach his eyes. "You are so much more intelligent than I gave you credit for, Chloe, you know that? I mean, how many times did Jonathan Byrd try to kill you? Twice? I underestimated you." He stood again, rounding behind the solid surface keeping her upright. Old hinges protested as he lifted the lid, but she couldn't force her neck to twist around in order for her to keep him in her vision. "Before coming to Colorado, I was the top cardiothoracic surgeon at the Mayo Clinic. I had it made. For seven long years, I saved hundreds of patients. I literally held their lives in my hands. I got to decide how long they had left on earth, whether they would see their children again, their grandchildren. That feeling of…playing God, it's very addictive, you know."

Chloe pulled against the zip ties. She narrowed her gaze as the clouds rolled above and exposed a sliver of sunlight. Her fingers brushed against cool metal, and her heart stalled in her throat. Craning her chin over one shoulder, she took in the pale blue color of the container at her back. No. He… he wouldn't. Her mouth dried on a sharp inhale, and she struggled against the binds again. The zip tie around her ankles would break under pressure, but she wasn't strong enough to break the plastic around her wrists. Not without injuring herself in the process. The lid compromised his view of her. It was now or never.

She brought her knees into her chest, the heels of her boots right against her pelvic bone. She splayed her knees out to either side as hard and as fast as she could. The zip tie around her ankle snapped, and she quickly pressed her knees together in case Michael had heard. She had to keep him talking, distracted. Using one foot, she pushed the broken tie to the outside of her hip. She forced her right shoulder to stretch as much as possible, and her fingers clawed into frozen dirt to get a hold of the tie. It slipped out of reach. Damn it. She tried again. "You made a mistake?"

"Too many." The distinct scent of bleach burned in her lungs. Footsteps echoed from behind as Michael rounded into her peripheral vision, a soaked rag in hand, and she forced herself to relax, but odor permeated her senses. Wind lifted his hair as he stared down at her. His eyes glazed slightly, as though remembering some distant memory, and Chloe tried for the broken zip tie again. "I am a senator's son. If the truth had gotten out, the media would've been all over it. I'd become the black sheep of my family, the embarrassment. I couldn't let that happen. Not with millions of dollars of inheritance at stake. The heart and vascular center was my last option."

"You left your history with the Mayo Clinic off your résumé. You lied about saving lives in third world countries so we wouldn't look too closely." Dread pooled at the base of her spine. She'd hired a narcissist with a God complex, worked beside him, trusted him. Chloe curled the broken zip tie into her palm, then made quick work of angling it under the bind around her wrist. She gripped both ends in her hands and pressed her thumb into the center of the tie, working it back and forth against the other. She'd gauged his height to be around six-foot-two, maybe six-foot-three, but he had more than eighty pounds on her. It wouldn't be hard for him to subdue her if she ran. "And when you left that clamp in Miriam Byrd's chest, you altered her chart to make sure no one else discovered what you did. All for money?"

Those dark eyes centered on her, and a stiffness infused the tendons between his shoulders and neck. Faster than she thought possible, Michael shot one hand out and wrenched her to her feet. "You of all people should understand I did what I had to do, Dr. Miles, and I'll keep doing it as long as I have the chance to save the people who would die if it weren't for me."

"How many people other than Miriam Byrd died because of you? Two? Three? Including the officer at the roadblock? You don't give a damn about our patients. This is all about your ego." Heat climbed into her face at the thought of this monster holding another life in his hands, hers included. The weakened zip ties around her wrists broke under pressure, and Chloe swayed forward to keep Michael off balance. "And there's no way in hell I'm letting you get away with it."

She wound one foot behind his and shoved him as hard as she could. Michael hit the dirt, and she ran. The mountain sloped down, directing her back toward town. Branches scratched against her face, just as they had in the woods near her home in Denver, only this time the fear didn't get to control her. Because she wasn't alone.

Weston Ford hadn't just been her partner during the course of this investigation. He'd become so much more. A friend, a trusted ally, a lover. In a matter of days, he'd stripped away her isolated existence and showed her what really mattered. Family. James Ford had given his life for her, Easton Ford had dedicated himself to solving this case for her and Karie Ford had stood as a testament of true loyalty for her. She'd come into Battle Mountain alone, afraid and detached, but she wasn't that person anymore. Because of them.

Chloe wound through a minefield of loose rocks and knee-high grass, not daring to turn around. Her breath sawed in and out of her chest. Adrenaline drained, and her body slowed despite her internal fight to keep going. She'd been running on fumes for days. She wasn't going to make it. Taking cover behind a large pine, she tried to disappear into its branches. A woodpecker carved a new hole into the bark overhead, masking all other sounds of the woods. No movement. No sign Michael had followed her. Keeping her gaze locked in the direction she'd come from, she stepped backward down the slope.

And met a wall of muscle.

She twisted around, her fist connecting with one side of his jaw, but it wasn't enough. Massive arms encircled her rib cage and squeezed the air from her lungs.

"I've come too far to let you ruin this for me now," Michael said.

The edges of her vision darkened. She kicked out to throw him off balance and shot her hands back to claw at his face as he hauled her back up the incline. The light blue refrigerator came into view, and every cell in her body screamed in protest. Chloe fought harder, burning precious oxygen as Michael forced her into the too small space.

"I really wish you'd held up your end of the deal." He sealed her inside.

THE FRONT PASSENGER door stood ajar.

Weston struggled to stay on his feet as he approached the small four-door sedan Chloe had used to escape town less than an hour ago. It had become a crime scene. His boots echoed off the pavement.

EMTs had already assessed the Silverton PD officer assigned to the roadblock.

According to his statement, he'd stopped Chloe Pascale to search her vehicle when a second vehicle had pulled up behind her. She looked as though she were under duress, crying, which had given the officer reason to search the car. The second driver had honked, as though in a hurry, and before the officer had any indication of what was happening, he was knocked unconscious from behind.

Now she was gone.

The weight of the Silverton and Creed PD officers' unspoken questions weighed heavy as he handled the driver's side door with gloves. Chloe wouldn't have left the vehicle voluntarily, which meant her abductor had to have taken her by force. The window had been rolled down, presumably for her to hand her license and registration to the Silverton officer when she'd been stopped. "I want prints taken from the door handle and the frame, and everything in this car bagged as evidence."

The officers moved on his orders.

He searched for something—anything—to tell him what'd happened in those few terrorizing seconds leading up to Chloe's abduction, but there was no telling how long the debris on the floorboards had been there. This wasn't her vehicle. They'd borrowed it from Macie, and without his dispatcher here to tell him exactly when each and every crumb had appeared in the vehicle, they were dead in the water.

He sat in the driver's seat and closed the door behind him. Twisting the keys in the ignition, he scanned the dashboard and steering column. The car instantly pinged with a warning light. One of the doors hadn't properly closed. He checked the driver's side again. Secure. Which meant… A sliver of sunlight outlined the seam of the passenger door. Her abductor wouldn't have gotten behind the wheel, but he would've had to reach inside if Chloe tried to escape out the other side.

Weston stretched the length of the car and reached for the opposite handle. "If she was over here, you would've grabbed her feet. Maybe she kicked you to get away." The scene played out in his head as though it were happening right in front of him, and a howling rage consumed him from head to toe. Damn it. Chloe had known there was another killer out here, that the bastard had tortured and killed Jonathan Byrd for information. Why the hell had she run?

He pulled his flashlight from his belt and hit the power button. Shadows fled the crevasses between the two front seats and the middle shifting column. With Jonathan Byrd decomposing on the exam table at the Jacob Family Funeral Home, he was back to his original suspect list. Someone who'd tried to stop Chloe from reporting the real reason Miriam Byrd had died after routine surgery four months ago to the board at the clinic.

The flashlight beam revealed a drop of liquid, and Weston moved in to get a better look. Blood. Impossible to tell whether or not it belonged to their suspect or Chloe, but from the location, his instincts said they had a direct link between her abduction and the bastard who'd skewered Jonathan Byrd. Chloe had fought back. "We've got blood. Hand me a bag and a swab."

"Here you go, Chief," one of the officers said.

Weston collected the evidence and sealed it into an evidence bag. He moved to pull out of the car, brushing against Macie's oversize key chain, and froze. An ache radiated down his arm as he set most of his weight into his free hand and wrist and reached for a shiny rectangular pin facedown against the floorboards. He pinched the pushpin between his index finger and thumb and turned it over. An American flag. It must've popped loose during the struggle, but Chloe hadn't been wearing it when she'd left the funeral home, which meant… "Son of a bitch."

He'd been right to suspect the bastard from the beginning. Weston extricated himself from the car. Handing off the pin to one of Creed's officers, he stripped the gloves from his hands and shoved them in his pockets. "Listen up!" All eyes shifted to him. "Our missing woman is Battle Mountain's coroner,

Chloe Pascale. Your captains should've forwarded all of you her driver's license photo. Only her real name is Chloe Miles, a cardiothoracic surgeon out of Denver. I have reason to believe one of her fellow surgeons, Dr. Michael Kerr, is responsible for what happened here today. He's already suspected of torturing and killing one man in the past twelve hours and injuring one of our officers." Weston faced the two officers to his right dressed in dark blue uniforms. "Silverton PD, I want you to go through DMV records and narrow down the make and model of Dr. Kerr's vehicle. After that, check in with all of the car rental agencies out of Denver to see if he decided to road trip with a vehicle that couldn't be linked to him. Canvass the town, talk to anyone you have to. We need to find that car."

He turned toward the three officers dressed in black. "Creed PD, you're with me. This killer is intelligent and desperate to cover his tracks. There's a chance he'll try to use an MO we picked up at the start of this case to place blame on a dead man by burying Chloe alive. We're looking for a '50s-style refrigerator. He'll stay within the boundaries our original killer set to strengthen our case. That leaves Contention Mine and the woods around it where Chloe and I discovered the first victim. Let's move."

He wasn't sure about any of it, but his instincts said Michael Kerr would do whatever it took to keep his involvement in this case as murky as possible.

Weston jogged around the hood of his brother's truck and turned back toward town. Adrenaline spiked his heart rate higher, and he drummed his fingers against the steering wheel as he and the two Creed patrol cruisers behind him tore back toward town.

She was alive. He had to believe that. He had to believe she would do everything to survive, to come back to him. Because he loved her, damn it. He hadn't been willing to see it before, but it was impossible to ignore now. He'd convinced himself he'd never find a partner to support him, to love him, after Cynthia had died. He'd accepted the fact, at some point, whomever he committed himself to would leave as she had, as his father had, as Easton had, hell, even as Chloe had, and he'd be left behind. Alone. Empty. But as he floored the accelerator to the opposite end of town and up the mountain, there was a certain clarity that drove straight into his chest.

Cynthia had let go to ease their combined suffering.

James Ford had sacrificed his life to save a practical stranger.

Easton had sacrificed his mental health for the greater good.

And Chloe… She'd sacrificed herself to protect him.

The people he'd come to rely on the most—who'd shaken his sense of security—had all put the lives of those they cared about before their own. Chloe had taken in the violence, the cruelty, of Jonathan Byrd's murder, and had chosen to draw the threat away from him, his family and away from the town he called home. And he loved her for it. Loved her protectiveness, her persistence and her strength, and he wasn't going to stop looking for her.

Main Street blurred in his peripheral vision as he led the way across town. Weston gripped the steering wheel harder as the truck's shocks absorbed the first climb up the dirt road leading to the mine where he'd discovered Whitney Avgerpoulos's body. This was where the investigation had started. Seemed only fitting this was where it would end. "Hang on, Doc. I'm coming."

The patrol cruisers cut their lights and sirens, dirt kicking up behind each one of them as the convoy ascended the mountain. Branches and leaves scraped against the side of Easton's truck, but Weston couldn't worry about the damage right then. The hood bounced as he forced the vehicle higher, then dipped just as the ground leveled out.

The tail of a dark pickup truck lodged into a grove of pines demanded attention. Weston skidded to a stop and slammed the truck into Park. In the same breath, he hit the dirt and unholstered his sidearm. Both officers left the safety of their patrol vehicles and followed his hand signals to approach the passenger side of the truck while he approached the driver's side. His wobbly reflection glared back at him from the tinted windows as he kept low and moved fast. Unhitching the door, he swung it open.

Empty.

"Check the registration and run these plates." Weston maneuvered toward the bed of the truck and scanned the patterns in the frozen dirt. Two depressed lines, about a foot apart, had been carved into the ground. Smooth and consistent. No tire tracks, but he was willing to bet Michael Kerr had borrowed the dolly Jonathan Byrd had used to get his victim's '50s-style coffins in place. He followed the tracks that disappeared opposite the small clearing in front of the mine, and his gut kicked hard.

He wasn't as familiar with these woods as he was with the land in and around his family's property, but the same rules applied. Determine the target, memorize a map of the area, know the dangers of going in on foot. Weston traced the dolly's tracks through the underbrush and scanned ahead. The clouds shifted overhead and shadows crawled up the mountain. Light brown rock stared back at him as he mentally matched the landscape to the map in his head. Michael Kerr wouldn't have been able to carry his victim and push the refrigerator up this incline at the same time. This was premeditated. He'd come into town for one thing: Chloe.

His chest tightened. Weston checked his weapon to ensure he'd loaded a round into the chamber. He called over his shoulder to the two Creed officers running the truck's VIN number. "One of you with me. We're going hunting."

Chapter Fourteen

It was so dark.

Chloe ran her bandaged hands over the inside frame of the refrigerator, her breath coming in small bursts. Her fingers grazed over the rubber seal along one side, but no matter how many times she'd tried, the lid wouldn't budge. Michael had already buried her. The more she panicked, the faster she'd burn through what little air she had left.

She wasn't sure how long she'd been locked inside. Time had no meaning in the darkness. A soft moan escaped up her throat, and she closed her eyes. Weston and Easton had escaped the freezer Jonathan Byrd buried them in. She could get herself free. She just had to calm down. She had to think. Her soft exhale filled her ears, but her heart rate only notched higher. "Come on."

Slow, shallow breaths. Of course, the Ford brothers had had each other. They were stronger. They'd worked together. She kept in shape to stay on the run. Running, Olympic lifting, yoga. If she could squat over one hundred pounds, she could wedge her feet against the lid and get the damn thing open. She just had to try.

Chloe brought her knees into her chest, setting her boots against the lid. Her knees dug into her rib cage, and she automatically held her breath to pressurize the air in her lungs as though she were getting ready to lift. Only this time, she was fighting for her life. Not a personal record. She hadn't heard a chain or a padlock put into place when Michael sealed her inside. She focused the majority of her strength in her heels and pushed against the lid with everything she had.

The door lifted slightly, but a waterfall of dirt cascaded down into the refrigerator. She covered her face against the onslaught and turned away from the avalanche more likely to suffocate her than give her a way to escape. The lid settled back into place. A sob thickened in her throat as she streaked her hands down her face. It was no use. She could raise the lid, but she'd only manage to kill herself in the process. She couldn't open it completely and climb through the several tons of dirt crushing down on her. She was going to die here.

Weston.

His name materialized at the front of her mind, and a calm settled over her. The wishful part of her brain tried to convince her he'd found Macie's vehicle at the roadblock outside town, that the officer who Michael Kerr had knocked unconscious had come around and called in her abduction. It wanted to convince her he was doing everything in his power to find her, despite the fact she'd run. But the logical part of her brain, the one she'd relied on these past few months to stay alive, said no one was coming to save her. She believed in heroes, but she had to save herself.

Dirt caked the inside of her mouth as she searched her pockets. Michael hadn't emptied her coat before wrestling her into the refrigerator, and he hadn't noticed she'd emptied his when he'd captured her in the trees. She unpocketed the phone she'd taken from him. No service. The screen automatically lit up, and relief coursed through her as the slightest hint of light chased back the blackness. It wasn't much. It wasn't anything, really, but the agitation knotting in her stomach released.

Until the low battery warning flashed across the screen.

Her single lifeline of comfort was running out. Tears blurred in her vision as the phone went into automatic battery saving mode. The screen dimmed, but there was still enough light for her to get a measure of the refrigerator. "It's okay. You can do this."

Setting the phone up against the left wall, Chloe shifted to her right and turned onto her side. There wasn't a whole lot of room to maneuver. She had the strength to lift the lid, but without something to protect her face, the massive amount of dirt on top of her would suffocate her before she had a chance to escape. As much as she wanted to believe Weston had learned about what'd occurred at the roadblock, she couldn't rely on him this time. He wasn't the type of man or police chief to ignore one of his residents in danger—no matter the emotional repercussions— but hope wasn't a plan.

She tugged her coat cuff over her hand to wiggle free from one sleeve. Her elbow slammed into the opposite wall and triggered nerve pain straight down to her fingers. A groan escaped past her mouth, but she caught herself to hold on to as much air for as long as possible. Moving slower than she wanted to go, she slipped free of her left sleeve and settled onto her back. Time for the other side. Her heart thumped hard behind her rib cage, starved for oxygen. Her hand slipped free of the other sleeve. Cold from the plastic interior burrowed under her shirt. She couldn't stop the shiver from the abrupt change in temperature.

Spring had barely fallen across Battle Mountain, but out here, deep within the earth, the ground was still frozen, barren and lonely. Tremors worked through her hands as she raised her hips and pulled her coat out from beneath her weight. She didn't want to be alone anymore, didn't want to die. Despite the paralyzing fear of realizing not one but two killers had targeted her, she felt more cared for, loved even, than she ever had in Denver, surrounded by friends and what little remained of her family. The people here had taken her in, but Weston Ford had given her something she'd never imagined she'd feel again: a future. She wasn't ready to give that up. Not as long as she still had air in her lungs.

She'd have to move fast. Dirt and pebbles scratched at her skin as she leveraged her feet against the lid again. The second she opened the door, another round of dirt and rock would fill the empty space and bury her. Threading her arms through opposite sleeves, she ducked her head beneath the hood of her coat to protect her face and eyes.

She had one shot. Her last chance. One breath. Two.

She filled her lungs as fast as possible and shoved everything she had into the heels of her feet. Soreness echoed down her right side from being thrown from the four-wheeler, but the lid lifted. Another wave of dirt rolled into the space and displaced the precious oxygen she coveted. Dirt covered her almost instantly, and she struggled to keep the lid open while trying to sit up at the same time. The ticking of rock hitting the plastic filled her ears. She stretched out one hand, locking her elbow against the weight of the door, and felt for the cracked seal with the other. She tunneled through the wall of dirt slowly burying her alive and gripped the edge of the door. Yes!

Pressure built in her chest the longer she held her breath, but she couldn't afford to exhale. Not yet. Sweat beaded in her hairline as she lowered one leg, then the other. The door closed on her opposite hand, but the pain was nothing compared to the alternative of suffocation. Her heels hit dirt that had collected in the appliance. She dug her chest, face and thighs out from under the weight of loose soil and twisted onto her knees. The bones in her fingers trapped between the heavy door and the seal shattered under the weight, but she couldn't cry out. Couldn't scream. Her nervous system's automatic survival messages would force her to breathe if she lost consciousness. She had to stay awake. She had to keep going.

Rocks bit into her knees through her jeans as she set her shoulders against the door, but she couldn't leverage her feet under her with so much of the refrigerator's space eaten up by earth. Time was running out. Despite the fact she couldn't see anything, granules of light prickled at the edges of her vision. She was going to pass out. Her heartbeat pulsed at the base of her skull. No. Not yet. Her head swam. Sliding her free hand down her left leg, she forced her boot through the dirt beneath her and tossed several inches to the bottom of the fridge. She could do this. She had to do this. She did the same for her left foot and had enough balance to thrust her shoulders against the weighted door.

A scream burst from her chest at the effort. Her lungs spasmed for air, but all she managed was a fraction of what she needed. The hood of her coat suctioned into her mouth. She was out of time. She couldn't hold the door open and climb through the opening at the same time. Her legs shook from the exertion, but she didn't have a choice. With the fingers of her right hand certainly broken, she clawed at the dirt still cascading into the refrigerator with the other. She couldn't breathe, couldn't think.

There was no way out.

Panic gripped like a tight vise around her heart. She was pulling in less and less air, her struggled inhales the only sound cutting through the silence. No. No, no, no, no. This wasn't how it was supposed to be. A wave of agony arced through her feet and up her legs. Her pulse shot into dangerous territory. Her heart was trying to get as much oxygen to the rest of her body as fast as possible, killing her while trying to save her.

She set her legs hip distance as best she could and raised the door another few inches. Pain radiated through her entire body as she gauged how many feet of soil she'd have to wade through to reach the surface. Her fingers tingled, her jaw ached from carrying the weight of the world on her shoulders. Literally. Tears burned down her face. The door lifted wider, but not wide enough for her to squeeze through. More dirt fell inside and surrounded her shins, and her strength ran out.

Her knees buckled, and the door collapsed closed. "No!"

WESTON AND THE Creed PD officer at his heels kept their distance from the set of tire tracks carved through the dirt. The killer had dragged Chloe and whatever he'd hauled on the dolly away from the mine for a reason. Chances were he'd come back this way when he was finished. Only Weston wasn't going to wait.

Sweat built in his palms as he crept along the man-made trail. The son of a bitch couldn't have gone far with such a heavy load, but he wouldn't want her found quickly, either. Branches swayed ahead, and Weston slowed, signaling the officer at his back to stop. Gusts of wind whistled through the passes above, but his instincts warned him he and his backup weren't alone anymore.

A gunshot exploded.

The rock to the right of his head caught the bullet and spit a veil of dust into his face. Weston twisted back to keep the obstruction between him and the shooter, but another bullet ripped through the trees and pegged the Creed officer. His backup went down, a groan following the echo bouncing off the peaks. Weston fisted the man's jacket and dragged him behind a boulder twenty feet back the way they'd come. Damn it. It was an ambush.

Chloe's abductor had been waiting for them.

Which meant he'd finished with his latest victim.

"Hang tight. Help is on the way." Crouching behind the boulder, Weston ripped his radio from his belt and pinched the push-to-talk button. "Dispatch, this is Ford. I'm taking fire near the entrance to Contention Mine. One shooter. Officer down. I repeat, officer down. Requesting Silverton and Creed backup as soon as possible."

Static filled the airwaves as Weston struggled to catch his breath. No movement. No sign the shooter had moved to get a better angle. The officer he'd left behind with Michael Kerr's truck would've heard the shots, but he couldn't leave the man at his feet to bleed out alone.

"Say again… Chief. Say—" Macie's voice dissolved.

Survival instinct bled into frustration. They were positioned between two peaks. The signal couldn't penetrate through the rock. Weston crouched beside the officer and pressed his palm into the bullet wound in the man's shoulder. Blood trickled up through his fingers and down the officer's uniform. Nichols, according to the nameplate pinned to the left side of his chest. "I'm going to get you out of here."

"You need to keep pressure on that wound," an

unfamiliar voice said. "Otherwise, there's a chance your friend there will bleed out."

Weston ripped his bloodied hand from his fellow officer and raised his weapon, taking aim. Dr. Michael Kerr, the resident surgeon who'd assisted Chloe during the life-ending surgery of Miriam Byrd, stepped into view, a revolver pointed straight back at him. "Battle Mountain PD, put the weapon down. Now!"

A low laugh punctured through the groan coming from the officer at his feet as Michael Kerr took another step forward. A high widow's peak disappeared under a layer of hair whipped across the man's forehead, a few days' worth of beard growth shadowing an otherwise smooth face. "You're not going to shoot me, Chief Ford. Because I'm the only one who knows where she is." Kerr shook his head and took another step forward. "No. What you're going to do is let me walk back to my truck, drive down this mountain and out of this pathetic town, forget I was ever here, and no one else has to get hurt."

"You son of a bitch. You wanted her dead all along. You encouraged Jonathan Byrd to find her after you told him the truth about what happened to his wife, didn't you? But you couldn't risk him coming after you. You would've had to have done it anonymously. What'd you do? Get a copy of Chloe's findings when she did the autopsy and send it to him?" His shoulders ached from holding his weapon steady, but he wouldn't let this bastard get away with what he'd done. "You knew she was going to go to the clinic's board and tell them everything, and you couldn't risk being named in the malpractice suit. You used your mother's connections to find her, told Jonathan Byrd where she was hiding. Can't imagine what the senator might lose if her son was implicated in the wrongful death of a patient." Weston noted the slight crease in Kerr's mouth. He'd struck a chord. "You blamed Chloe for the mistake during that surgery. You used Jonathan Byrd like a weapon, and then you pointed him at Roberta Ellis and Chloe. All to save yourself, but something went wrong."

Kerr didn't answer, didn't even seem to breathe as his gaze flickered to the officer he'd shot at Weston's feet. The killer fanned his grip over the revolver in his hand.

"You lost control of your pet project. Jonathan Byrd was angry enough to kill anyone involved in his wife's death, but you couldn't afford his actions to link back to you or for him to catch you by surprise." Seconds ticked off in his head, each stacking against the one before it. "You had to put him down like the rabid dog you'd turned him into."

"That's a great story, Chief, but that's all it is. A story you'll never be able to prove, and the longer you try, the faster Dr. Miles suffocates." Michael Kerr's gun lowered a fraction. The man was a surgeon. While he saved and destroyed lives with a steady hand, he'd most likely never trained with weapons as long as Weston had. His arm was getting tired.

"You sure about that?" Weston nodded toward the small piece of gauze and tape wrapped between Kerr's thumb and index finger on his right hand behind the gun's grip. "Because the way Chloe saw it, whoever tortured Jonathan Byrd stabbed him with so much force, his hand slipped down the handle of the scalpel. The interim coroner is collecting samples from the remains right now. What are the chances the victim's DNA isn't the only blood the lab finds or that we won't be able to tie the clamp Chloe removed from Miriam Byrd's remains back to you?"

Shock smoothed Kerr's expression.

"That's right, Kerr. She outsmarted you, but you still have one bargaining chip here." Every muscle down his spine hardened with battle-ready tension, and Weston was the one to take a step forward this time. "Tell me where she is, and the district attorney might take your cooperation into consideration when filing charges for three counts of conspiracy to commit murder and first-degree murder."

"You remember the part where I said I'm walking out of here, Chief? Nobody is taking this from me. Not even you. Now you can get out of my way, or you can die as slowly and painfully as she is right now." Michael Kerr pulled the trigger.

The gun jammed, but faster than Weston thought possible the killer threw the weapon straight at him. Steel struck the side of his head, and he wrenched back, losing his aim. Pain splintered across his temple. Kerr lunged. Jumping off a rock between them, his attacker got the upper hand and swung a hard right hook. Lightning struck behind his eyes, and his weapon discharged a split second before Kerr knocked it from his hand. A solid kick to the sternum thrust him into the rock at his back. Strong hands wrapped around his throat and pushed him down. His knees threatened to collapse out from under him as Weston spotted his weapon a few feet away.

The wounded officer had lost consciousness. Chloe had been buried alive. Backup had no idea where he was.

Pure survival twisted Kerr's face into something unrecognizable, and a thread of spittle hung from dry, cracked lips. "Did you know seventy percent of strangulation victims are found with a broken hyoid bone? You see, it all depends on your age, the shape of the hyoid and whether or not the hyoid synchondrosis have fused. I wonder how much pressure it'll take to break yours."

His heart thudded loud behind his ears as he tried to breathe through the grip around his throat.

Weston dug his hands into the man's forearms. The clock ticking at the back of his mind intensified. Chloe. She was out here, alone, afraid, dying. He wasn't going to lose her. Not again.

Weston released his hold on Kerr. He didn't know anything about human anatomy, but he'd gotten into plenty of fights with Easton to strike where it hurt. He rocketed his knee into Kerr's left kidney. The pressure around his throat released, and he gasped for air. His vision wavered, but he didn't let it stop him from fisting what was left of Kerr's hair. He slammed his knee into the bastard's face, and the good doctor collapsed. Unconscious. "Wonder which bones of yours are broken now."

He struggled to catch his breath. He wiped the blood from his temple with the back of his hand and collected his weapon. Flipping Michael Kerr onto his face, Weston handcuffed him to the downed officer, whose pulse was still strong, just as his partner exploded through the trees, weapon raised. "I've got an officer down and one suspect in custody. Call it in!"

Weston didn't wait for confirmation as he retargeted the dolly tracks he'd followed into the woods and headed up the mountain. His body hurt, his throat raw. He protected his face against the branches clawing at his face, desperation drowning the burn in his lungs. The tracks wound through a thick grove of trees, and he burst through them, out of breath.

The tracks ended.

In their place, a disturbed area of loose soil. Just as he'd noted before finding Whitney Avgerpoulos's remains. Weston collapsed to his knees and started digging. "Chloe!"

Dirt packed under his fingernails and numbed his hands. Blood dripped into the soil underneath him. Every cell in his body caught fire as he uncovered the smooth metal of a refrigerator too small for even her to survive inside. Weston repositioned himself to the longest side of the container, his boot striking a shovel discarded in the weeds. He made quick work of digging around the perimeter of the refrigerator and tossed the shovel. His hands blistered from the combination of dried wood and the sheen of sweat on his palms, but he didn't stop. Kneeling into the moat he'd created along one side, he hauled the door above his head.

A single pale hand reached toward the surface, her fingers swelling at odd angles. Broken. Unmoving. He worked faster, harder, unburying her inch by agonizing inch from the dirt that'd filled the refrigerator. "Hang on, baby. Hang on!"

He freed her left arm and scrambled to uncover her head and shoulders. Her coat crumpled as his hands tangled in long brown hair, and his heart stopped. She'd covered her face with the hood of her jacket to keep the dirt from choking her. She'd tried to escape. Weston pushed his hands beneath the loose soil and positioned his arms beneath hers, pulling her from her makeshift coffin.

"Come on, Doc. Don't you dare die on me. Don't let him win." Lowering the hood from her face, he smoothed her hair back. Streaks of dirt marred her complexion. He set his ear against her perfect mouth. No breathing sounds. Laying her flat, Weston interlaced his hands and centered the base of his palms beneath her sternum and compressed. "One, two, three, four." He set his mouth against hers and breathed every ounce of desperation, hope and love into her lungs, then got back to chest compressions. "Wake up, Chloe. You and I aren't finished. We'll never be finished."

Chloe's back arched off the ground as she gasped for air.

Chapter Fifteen

Coming back to life hurt more than she expected.

It was nothing compared to the ache of slowly suffocating to death, but she'd take any kind of pain she could get at this point. It was better than feeling nothing at all.

Chloe huddled into the space blanket provided by the EMT who'd stayed behind for her as she recounted to one of the Silverton PD officers what'd happened after her abduction at the roadblock. Pines swayed against the constant hum and whistle of wind, and a shiver chased down her spine. The truck bed of Easton's pickup bounced as the tech wrapping her broken fingers in splints maneuvered around for supplies. Sunlight glared off the light brown rocks of the peaks demanding attention outside Contention Mine. Four days ago, she'd responded to a call from the Battle Mountain PD dispatcher, which had set this nightmare in motion. Here she was, outside that same mine, alive in the end. These trees, these mountains—they'd stood the test of that time, but everything had changed. Exhaustion stole the last of her energy, and she settled against the cold steel of the truck bed.

Dirt crusted her hairline and fell in uneven batches with every movement. The idea to keep her coat over her face as she'd fought to escape the refrigerator had kept the soil out of her mouth, nose and lungs, but it had worked beneath her clothing and stuck to everything else in the worst way possible. The short hours she and Weston had spent in the tree house she'd vowed to hate seemed like a lifetime ago. What she wouldn't give for a hot shower and the comforting scent of the honey soap she'd used there, for the thick robe and the warm man against her.

Her hands shook despite the blanket draped over her. She'd treated enough patients during her ER rotation as a med student to watch for signs of shock, but it would still be another thirty minutes, at least, before the EMT would clear her. The officer who'd been shot had been rushed to a full-service hospital in Grand Junction in the town's only ambulance. She'd have to wait, but the fact she was still breathing said she'd walk away from the scene on her own two feet. The EMT explained there would be chest pain over the next few days as her body adjusted to the lack of oxygen over a sustained period of time, but her vitals were steady. She would live.

The scene buzzed with controlled chaos as three different police departments collected evidence and put the last pieces of the investigation on paper. It was over. Jonathan Byrd's remains had been collected by the coroner out of Creed, and the samples Easton Ford and the interim coroner had taken from the body were already on their way to the lab in Denver for testing. Considering the amount of force it'd taken for the killer to drive a scalpel into Jonathan Byrd's bone, the lab would most assuredly find DNA that forensically identified who had wielded the scalpel that'd killed her attacker. But there was no doubt in her mind—Dr. Michael Kerr's blood would match.

Anxiety coiled in her stomach as two officers, one being the unforgettable man who'd pulled her from her own grave, escorted her former colleague to a waiting police cruiser. The officer Michael Kerr had knocked unconscious at the roadblock had quickly identified the vehicle of his attacker as a dark blue pickup, matching the rental the disgraced surgeon had used to abduct her and transport the refrigerator he'd buried her inside. Preliminary ballistics had already compared the bullet recovered from Jonathan Byrd's head wound and the last bullets found in Kerr's gun. They were a visual match.

A man she'd worked beside for years would be charged with first-degree murder, attempted murder and three counts of conspiracy to commit murder.

While he hadn't killed Roberta Ellis or Whitney Avgerpoulos, he'd enlisted a grieving husband to do the work for him. He'd spend the rest of his life behind bars and lose any claim to his family's fortune. From what little Chloe had overheard from the Silverton officers a few feet away, Senator Kerr herself had already held a press conference to deny her knowledge of her son's actions and remove him from the family trust.

The heart and vascular clinic would hear the news soon. The truth would come out. Chloe and the rest of her surgical team who'd been in the operating room that day would be suspended until the investigation was complete. With Jonathan Byrd dead, his malpractice suit filed against her would be dismissed, but the board would be forced to investigate all of her other surgeries. The press alone would hurt the clinic and the patients who'd relied on their physicians to get them through the scariest times of their lives.

She was going to lose everything. Her medical career was over.

But with the thought came an undeniable peace. She'd planned to tell the board what'd happened to Miriam Byrd before her attack in Denver. She was going to take responsibility for Michael Kerr's mistake and step down as the head of her department. Only now, the man she thought would be replacing her would spend the rest of his life in prison.

She curled one hand into the reflective space blanket. Michael turned that dark gaze to her, and her heart rate kicked behind her ribs. She forced her blistered hand to relax as Weston blocked her killer's line of sight, and the uneasiness from having to face her attacker eased. Because of him. The police chief who'd never given up on her, even when he'd had the chance.

Weston settled both hands on his waist, his back to her, as the other officer pushed Michael Kerr into his seat. The patrol car's siren chirped once as it pulled out of the small clearing and headed down the mountain back toward town. She wasn't sure what would happen to the surgeon now. Once she handed over the clamp she'd removed from Miriam Byrd's remains and all the forensic evidence had been verified, the state would presumably have Michael transferred to a larger holding facility, possibly back in Denver, while the district attorney filed official charges.

Battle Mountain's police chief turned to face her, and the fear, the investigation, the mine—it all fell away as though it'd never existed. There was only Weston. Her partner. Her friend. Her everything. He closed the distance between them, and Chloe pulled away from the truck bed frame to sit straighter. "Fancy meeting you here, Doc." That crooked smile she hadn't known existed a few days ago punctured through the fear and isolation that usually controlled her, and she couldn't help but smile in return. "For the record, crime scenes are not my favorite place to bring dates."

"Is that what this is?" Her chest ached as a laugh escaped, and she set her hand over her sternum to hold herself together. In vain. She'd done nothing but try to keep herself from shattering into a million pieces since learning Roberta Ellis had been buried alive, but her control had worn thin. She was supposed to feel relieved—happy, even—they'd solved the case, but all that was left was…emptiness.

Concern wiped Weston's amusement from his expression, and he stepped into her. Placing one hand between her shoulder blades, he set the other over her hand on her chest. "Deep breaths, Doc. I've got you. Whatever you need, I'm here."

"Thank you." Chloe settled her forehead against his shoulder and matched her breathing to his. The softness of his flannel shirt warmed under her temple, and suddenly there was nothing she could do to stop the flood of terror and guilt she'd tried to bury at the back of her mind. A sob wracked through her. Tears streaked down her face, but Weston only held her tighter.

She was so tired. Tired of being someone she wasn't, of lying, of running, of merely surviving. She just wanted to go home. She wanted somewhere she could call home. Somewhere she could be herself, where the hardest part of her day would be figuring out what to make for dinner, and she didn't want to do it alone. She wanted a partner, someone she could trust, talk with, laugh. She wanted Weston. She wanted to be loved by him.

She brushed her unbroken fingers against Weston's collar and buried her nose against his neck. Committed, dependent, loyal. There wasn't an ounce of her that hadn't fallen in love with him over the course of this investigation, but her brain had locked on to the fact he wasn't ready to move on from his wife. Swiping at the dirt caking under her eyes, she forced herself to take a shaky breath and put some distance between them. "I'm sorry. I'm sure you don't want to stand here and get cried on."

"Don't ever apologize for feeling what you have to feel. The past few days have been harder on you than anyone else. Well, maybe not the people who were killed, but you get my point." Callused hands framed her jaw, and Weston urged her to look up at him despite what the two of them must look like to the officers still working the scene. He traced the top of her cheekbone with the pad of his thumb. "Besides, I never liked this shirt anyway."

He was trying to set her at ease, and it was working. Damn him. Her mouth tugged at one corner as the pressure of breaking his gaze won out over the moment. Chloe winced as she tried to bend her broken fingers around the edge of the space blanket. "I'm sure you have a lot of work to do here. You don't have to stay with me. I can wait for the ambulance to come back from Grand Junction or have the EMT drive me to the clinic."

"Chloe," he said, his voice dipping into dangerous territory. Her name on his lips urged her to bring her gaze to his. "Stop wasting your energy on trying to get rid of me. It's not going to work. I almost lost you out here. Again. I'm not going anywhere. Just tell me what you need from me."

A weightlessness slid through her at the sincerity in his voice, in his expression, in the way he held her as though he couldn't stand not to touch her, and the anxiety building in her stomach dissipated. A fresh round of hot tears welled in her eyes. "I need a shower, and a hot meal, and a nap, and for you to be there when I wake up."

Strong arms secured her against his chest, and Weston set his chin on the crown of her head. "Let's get you home."

Whitney Avgerpoulos was finally able to go home.

Home. That single world had a different meaning now.

Wasn't just where his phone connected to Wi-Fi automatically. It'd become so much more than that over the past few days. It'd become a person. Chloe. No matter where they went from here, he'd never look at the Whispering Pines the same again. Still, they needed somewhere to recover from the events of this investigation, and he doubted Chloe would be comfortable in his one-bedroom, one-bathroom apartment long. Especially given his limited cooking skills and men's hygiene products.

Denver PD was sending two detectives to Battle Mountain to review the recent investigation and officially close Dr. Roberta Ellis's case. The forensics lab wouldn't have the results from the tox screens or DNA evidence from each victim for another few days, but from what the district attorney had said, Michael Kerr and his public defender were already looking at making a deal. The senator's press conference had done its job in making it clear she hadn't known anything about her son's activities, that she and her staff had severed contact with the good doctor and that Kerr had forfeited his future inheritance.

The Silverton officer who'd been knocked unconscious during Chloe's abduction had officially put in his retirement papers, claiming he'd seen enough excitement in an otherwise uneventful career. While the officer who'd taken a bullet during the shoot-out had already tried to discharge himself early to get back on shift. Both had been invaluable to the investigation. Without them, he could've lost Chloe forever.

Weston pulled up the long drive, the shocks of his pickup doing their best to absorb the change in elevation. Didn't seem to bother the sleeping beauty in the passenger seat, whose ordeal had ended a mere twenty-four hours ago. He doubted a nuclear bomb could wake her now. He shoved the truck into Park as a single figure descended the main house's porch stairs. His heart protested at the absence of the family patriarch who'd always been at Karie Ford's side to greet him.

His mother folded her arms across her chest as he shouldered out of the truck, her usually quick smile waning. Her flannel shirt bellowed wide as she stretched her arms out. She brought him in for a too-tight hug before scanning him from head to toe as a mother often did. "Easton told me about what happened out at the mine." Her watery brown gaze shifted to the passenger in his truck as she pulled away. Long fingers with soft loose skin interlaced with his, and she patted the back of his hand. "That one of her fellow surgeons tried to bury her alive to save his own skin. Thank goodness you were there. How is she?"

"She's tired, overwhelmed by everything, but she's strong. She just needs a few days to recover. The DA says their case is solid. I've turned everything over to Denver PD, including the refrigerators from all three crime scenes and Jonathan Byrd's remains and the pickup truck he used to…" Weston swallowed to counter the thickness in his throat. "Chloe told them where they could find the clamp she hid from Michael Kerr, too. They were the ones to first catch the case. Makes sense they'd wrap it up."

What then? He couldn't stop the thought from worming its way into the front of his mind. With Jonathan Byrd dead and Michael Kerr headed for a life sentence behind bars, Chloe was safe. Free to go wherever she wanted. Whether that meant going back to her old life or including him in her decision, he had no idea, but nearly losing her like that had ripped open a part of him he believed lost after Cynthia passed. He didn't want to be alone anymore, but it was more than that. He needed Chloe in his life. This town needed her. Her confidence and temper, her softness and strength. Every cell in his body craved every cell in hers. Because he loved her. Weston turned to his mother. "How are you holding up?"

Karie shifted her weight, a familiar move when she wasn't comfortable with attention. "Oh, you know, your father took care of most everything around here. We built this place to raise our kids, but the income from tourists is what pays the bills, groceries and our…my health insurance." His mother slid her hand out of his, pulling her shoulders back. "Hard to imagine keeping it going without him. I don't really see any other option than to sell. Neither you nor your brother are in a position to help me run things around here." Her voice wavered. A strand of white hair blew in front of her face. "Easton's taken care of all the funeral arrangements for tomorrow, but sometimes I catch myself telling your father to come eat lunch or trying to show him a story in the paper. It's not real yet."

Karie Ford had stood as a strong example of fortitude and kindness all his life, but right then all Weston saw was a reflection of the same grief he'd suffered after losing Cynthia in his mother's eyes.

"I'm sorry, Mom." He encircled her in his arms. His heart lodged in his throat at the thought of her having to sell off the property he'd called home his entire life.

"Oh, honey, I don't blame you. For any of this. Your father made his choice. He knew what he was getting into going out there. He dedicated his life to helping those less fortunate or that couldn't help themselves. It's only fitting that's how he left. On his terms." She put a foot of distance between them, cleared her throat and swiped at her face. "Now you two get cleaned up and settled. I'll make sure you have something to eat when you're both ready."

"Thank you," he said.

His mother reached out, brushing the pad of her thumb across his cheek. "You remind me so much of him, Weston. Putting everyone else's needs and safety before your own. Just remember to put yourself first every once in a while." Karie's gaze slid to the passenger in his truck. "You deserve to be happy."

He nodded as she turned back toward the main cabin and ascended the stairs. Weston stared after her, seeing the cracks beginning to form as his mother tried to hold herself together. Losing a spouse changed a person, and finding that kind of support and love again was rare. Unless you were lucky enough for it to move into town unannounced and respond to a dead body. He rounded to the passenger side of the truck and opened the door softly. Setting his hand beneath Chloe's elbows, he took her weight against his chest and swung her legs up. "Come on, Doc. You're raining dirt."

"Where are we?" The question barely left her lips as more than a whisper.

"Home." He carried her across the property toward the satellite cabin he'd taken up during the investigation. As comfortable as he was in the one he and Cynthia had shared during her treatments, it was time to start something new, fresh. He'd never forget his wife. Hell, how could he forget someone who'd been such a large part of his past? His mother had been right. He deserved to move on, deserved to live, to be happy. The door swung inward, and Weston maneuvered her through the opening. "No offense, but you've smelled better."

Her laugh spiked his blood pressure higher as he set her in one of the chairs around the small kitchen table. "The people I work with don't care what I smell like."

"You mean because they're dead." He couldn't

help but smile as he slipped her boots from her feet and tossed them out the front door to contain the amount of dirt inside. Weston set his hands at the backs of her arms and pulled her upright into his chest. Right where she belonged. Pale green eyes gazed up at him as he smoothed her crusted hair away from her face, and her smile waned. He had to know where they stood, where they went from here. In that moment, his future stood on the edge of a blade. Tip it too far one direction and he'd lose everything. "Chloe, I know the case is closed and you have an entire life and career and friends back in Denver, but I—"

"I'm not going back to Denver." She reclaimed some of her own strength, although she seemed to still need help balancing. Her mouth curled at one corner as she set her hand over his heart. "I knew exactly what I was giving up when I ran three months ago. I knew I'd never be able to go back with my reputation intact or that I'd be able to pretend I hadn't been involved in the preventable death of a patient, even if it wasn't my fault. I convinced myself once this investigation was closed, I could still have that life, that I'd be happy."

His gut clenched as he prepared for the final blow.

"But I've built a better life here." She rolled her bottom lip between her teeth. "It sounds silly, but I like that Reagan remembers my name when I order coffee. I like that people smile at me when I walk down the street and bring me dinners for no apparent reason other than they made too much. I like my job and the people I work with at the funeral home, which sounds weird, but it's true. I feel more at home here than I've felt anywhere else. Battle Mountain isn't just the town I used to escape my past. It's my future, and I hope, with time, I can earn back the trust they've shown me these past few months." She fisted his shirt in her unbroken hand. "And I want you to be part of that future, Chief Ford. Late-night emergencies, family dinners, helping you and your mom maintain this place—I want it all. I want you. Forever."

"I love you, too." Warmth exploded through his chest as he crushed his mouth to hers. Weston threaded one hand through the rat's nest of her hair but quickly pulled back. "Does that future include a shower?"

"For the record, you didn't smell great either after you'd been buried in that freezer with your brother, but I pushed past it." She pressed her hand into his chest, forcing him across the cabin backward until he hit the closed bathroom door. Chloe notched her chin higher and leveled her mouth with his.

"You're right." He reached behind him and twisted the bathroom doorknob open. They fell in a tangle of limbs and surprised protests as Weston latched onto her hips. "I'll just hold my breath."

She swatted his arm as she whispered against his mouth. "Careful, Chief. Out of all the people in this town, I'm the one who knows where the bodies are buried."

Epilogue

Easton Ford folded his hands, one over the other, as he stood beside the coffin.

A bite of cold infused an already grim day as he, his brother and a few of his father's friends waited for the signal to carry the casket from the church down the short path to the cemetery.

His mother secured her hand in Chloe Miles's from the front row of pews, her skin too pale and streaked with tears. It seemed as though the entire town had come to pay their respects, a testament to how many lives James Ford had touched in his too-short sixty-three years. His father had been a great man, one who'd taught his sons loyalty, responsibility and, more importantly, duty to a man's town and family before himself.

Those same principles had gotten the old man killed.

Easton served his country believing his father had been right, and he'd lost everyone in his unit because of it. He held his head high as the pastor ended the service. He wrapped his grip around the handle and hefted the weight of his father's remains above his shoulder with the other men in the procession. This wasn't the first funeral he'd attended since coming home, and it wouldn't be the last, but as Battle Mountain's first reserve officer, he'd make damn sure he wouldn't be caught unprepared again.

* * * * *

WE HOPE YOU ENJOYED
THIS BOOK FROM

⊕ HARLEQUIN

INTRIGUE

Seek thrills. Solve crimes. Justice served.

Dive into action-packed stories that will keep you
on the edge of your seat. Solve the crime
and deliver justice at all costs.

6 NEW BOOKS AVAILABLE EVERY MONTH!

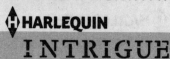
#2055 CONARD COUNTY: MISTAKEN IDENTITY
Conard County: The Next Generation • by Rachel Lee

In town to look after her teenage niece, Jasmine Nelson is constantly mistaken for her twin sister, Lily. When threatening letters arrive on Lily's doorstep, ex-soldier and neighbor Adam Ryder immediately steps in to protect Jazz. But will their fragile trust and deepest fears give the stalker a devastating advantage—one impossible to survive?

#2056 HELD HOSTAGE AT WHISKEY GULCH
The Outriders Series • by Elle James

To discover what real life is about, former Delta Force soldier Joseph "Irish" Monahan left the army and didn't plan to need his military skills ever again. But when a masked stalker attempts to murder Tessa Bolton, Irish is assigned as her bodyguard and won't abandon his mission to catch the killer *and* keep Tessa alive.

#2057 SERIAL SLAYER COLD CASE
A Tennessee Cold Case Story • by Lena Diaz

Still haunted by the serial killer she couldn't catch, police detective Bree Clark doesn't hesitate to accept PI Ryland Beck's offer of redemption. The Smoky Mountain Slayer cold case has gone hot again and working together could bring the murderer to justice. But is the culprit the original slayer—or a dangerous copycat?

#2058 MISSING AT FULL MOON MINE
Eagle Mountain: Search for Suspects • by Cindi Myers

Deputy Wes Landry knows he shouldn't get emotionally involved with his assignments. But a missing person case draws him to Rebecca Whitlow. Desperate to find her nephew, she's worried the rock climber has gotten lost...or worse. Something dangerous is happening at Full Moon Mine—and they're about to get caught in the thick of it.

#2059 DEAD GIVEAWAY
Defenders of Battle Mountain • by Nichole Severn

Deputy Easton Ford left Battle Mountain—and the woman who broke his heart—behind for good. Now his ex-fiancée, District Attorney Genevieve Alexander, is targeted by a killer, and he's the only man she trusts to protect her. But will his past secrets get them both killed?

#2060 MUSTANG CREEK MANHUNT
by Janice Kay Johnson

When his ex, Melinda McIntosh, is targeted by a paroled criminal, Sheriff Boyd Chaney refuses to let the stubborn officer be next on the murderer's revenge list. Officers and their loved ones are being murdered and danger is closing in. But will their resurrected partnership be enough to keep them safe?

SPECIAL EXCERPT FROM

⊕ HARLEQUIN
INTRIGUE

*Still haunted by the serial killer she couldn't catch, police
detective Bree Clark doesn't hesitate to accept
PI Ryland Beck's offer of redemption. The Smoky Mountain
Slayer cold case has gone hot again and working together
could bring the murderer to justice. But is the culprit the
original slayer—or a dangerous copycat?*

Read on for a sneak preview of
Serial Slayer Cold Case,
part of A Tennessee Cold Case Story series,
from Lena Diaz.

Chapter One

Maintaining a white-knuckle grip on the steering wheel while
negotiating the treacherous curves up Prescott Mountain on his
daily commute was typical for Ryland Beck. *Smiling* while he
resolutely refused to look toward the steep drop on the other
side of the road *wasn't* typical. Nothing, not even his phobia
of heights, could dampen his enthusiasm this chilly October
morning. Today he'd begin his investigation into a serial killer
case that had gone cold over four years ago.

Bringing down the Smoky Mountain Slayer was the challenge
of a lifetime. No suspects. No DNA. No viable behavioral
profile. In spite of the lack of evidence, Ryland was determined
to put the killer behind bars. He wanted to give the families of
the five victims the answers and justice they deserved.

Unfortunately, what he couldn't give them was closure.
Closure, as he well knew, was a fictional construct. The death of

a loved one would always leave a gaping hole in the hearts and lives of those left behind. But knowing the victim's murderer had been caught and punished would go a long way toward making the excruciating grief more bearable.

He continued winding his way up the mountain toward UB headquarters as he considered the limited information he'd found on the internet about the killings. The Slayer's modus operandi was consistent: all of his victims were strangled, their bodies dumped in the woods in Monroe County. But aside from them being young women, the victimology was all over the place. Their educational and economic backgrounds varied, as did their ethnicity. Some were married, some weren't. Some had children, some didn't. All of that made it nearly impossible to build a useful profile to help figure out who'd murdered them.

The detectives from the Monroe County Sheriff's Office had deemed the case unsolvable. But here in Gatlinburg, Ryland had a unique advantage: an über-wealthy boss who knew firsthand the suffering a victim's family endured when a murder case went cold.

Seven years after his wife was killed and his infant daughter went missing, Grayson Prescott had given up on the stagnant police investigation. He decided to create a cold case company called Unfinished Business. Just a few months later, UB had solved the case. Now, the thirty-three counties of the East Tennessee region had formed a partnership with UB and were clamoring for them to work their cold cases.

Don't miss
Serial Slayer Cold Case *by Lena Diaz,*
available March 2022 wherever
Harlequin books and ebooks are sold.

Harlequin.com

Get 4 FREE REWARDS!

We'll send you 2 FREE Books plus 2 FREE Mystery Gifts.

Harlequin Intrigue books are action-packed stories that will keep you on the edge of your seat. Solve the crime and deliver justice at all costs.

FREE Value Over $20

YES! Please send me 2 FREE Harlequin Intrigue novels and my 2 FREE gifts (gifts are worth about $10 retail). After receiving them, if I don't wish to receive any more books, I can return the shipping statement marked "cancel." If I don't cancel, I will receive 6 brand-new novels every month and be billed just $4.99 each for the regular-print edition or $5.99 each for the larger-print edition in the U.S., or $5.74 each for the regular-print edition or $6.49 each for the larger-print edition in Canada. That's a savings of at least 12% off the cover price! It's quite a bargain! Shipping and handling is just 50¢ per book in the U.S. and $1.25 per book in Canada.* I understand that accepting the 2 free books and gifts places me under no obligation to buy anything. I can always return a shipment and cancel at any time. The free books and gifts are mine to keep no matter what I decide.

Choose one: ☐ **Harlequin Intrigue Regular-Print** (182/382 HDN GNXC) ☐ **Harlequin Intrigue Larger-Print** (199/399 HDN GNXC)

Name (please print)

Address   Apt. #

City   State/Province   Zip/Postal Code

Email: Please check this box ☐ if you would like to receive newsletters and promotional emails from Harlequin Enterprises ULC and its affiliates. You can unsubscribe anytime.

Mail to the **Harlequin Reader Service:**
IN U.S.A.: P.O. Box 1341, Buffalo, NY 14240-8531
IN CANADA: P.O. Box 603, Fort Erie, Ontario L2A 5X3

Want to try 2 free books from another series? Call 1-800-873-8635 or visit www.ReaderService.com.

---

*Terms and prices subject to change without notice. Prices do not include sales taxes, which will be charged (if applicable) based on your state or country of residence. Canadian residents will be charged applicable taxes. Offer not valid in Quebec. This offer is limited to one order per household. Books received may not be as shown. Not valid for current subscribers to Harlequin Intrigue books. All orders subject to approval. Credit or debit balances in a customer's account(s) may be offset by any other outstanding balance owed by or to the customer. Please allow 4 to 6 weeks for delivery. Offer available while quantities last.

Your Privacy—Your information is being collected by Harlequin Enterprises ULC, operating as Harlequin Reader Service. For a complete summary of the information we collect, how we use this information and to whom it is disclosed, please visit our privacy notice located at corporate.harlequin.com/privacy-notice. From time to time we may also exchange your personal information with reputable third parties. If you wish to opt out of this sharing of your personal information, please visit readerservice.com/consumerschoice or call 1-800-873-8635. **Notice to California Residents**—Under California law, you have specific rights to control and access your data. For more information on these rights and how to exercise them, visit corporate.harlequin.com/california-privacy.

HI21R2

Marcus watched as she got to her feet. He was grateful to
see that she was steady.

"Can we have a minute?" Marcus asked Blade.

"Yeah. Hang on to her good arm," his friend replied.
Then he walked away, taking Dawson with him.

"What?" she asked, offering him a sweet smile.

"I'm going to find who did this. I promise you. And
you're going to be okay. Jamie Weathers is the best
emergency physician this side of the Colorado River.
Hell, this side of the Missouri River. He'll fix you up.
But don't leave the hospital until you hear from me. You
understand?"

"I got it," she said. "I'm going to be fine. It's all going to be fine. I barely had twenty bucks in my bag. He didn't even get my phone. I had that in my back pocket. Nor my keys. Those were in my hand. So he basically got nothing except the cash and my driver's license."

Things didn't matter. "You want me to let Brian and Morgan know?"

"Oh, God, no. Please don't do that." She looked panicked. "Morgan can't have stress right now. I'm grateful that her room is on the other side of the building. Otherwise, she could be watching this spectacle."

They would want to know. But it was her decision. And she was in pain. "Okay," he said, giving in easily.

"Thank you," she said.

"Go get fixed up. I'll talk to you soon."

She nodded.

"And, Erin…" he added.

"Yeah."

"I'm really glad that you're okay."

Don't miss
Trouble in Blue *by Beverly Long,*
available March 2022 wherever
Harlequin Romantic Suspense
books and ebooks are sold.

Harlequin.com

HRSEXP0122B